Cold Edge

Christmas in the Wind River Mountains of Wyoming.

A man named Joseph and a pregnant girl named Maria.

Three sheepmen and a Starr in the east.

The strangest priest who ever came to the frontier and his "daughter," who used to be a whore known as Angel.

And Edge. A loner who became a part of this scenario for a miracle without understanding why.

And whose presence inevitably triggered a chain reaction of violence that was to leave a ghastly trail of dead men's blood on the snow.

THE EDGE SERIES:

#1 THE LONER
#2 TEN GRAND
#3 APACHE DEATH
#4 KILLER'S BREED
#5 BLOOD ON SILVER
#6 RED RIVER
#7 CALIFORNIA KILL
#8 HELL'S SEVEN
#9 BLOODY SUMMER
#10 BLACK VENGEANCE
#11 SIOUX UPRISING
#12 DEATH'S BOUNTY
#13 THE HATED
#14 TIGER'S GOLD
#15 PARADISE LOSES
#16 THE FINAL SHOT
#17 VENGEANCE VALLEY
#18 TEN TOMBSTONES
#19 ASHES AND DUST
#20 SULLIVAN'S LAW
#21 RHAPSODY IN RED
#22 SLAUGHTER ROAD
#23 ECHOES OF WAR
#24 SLAUGHTERDAY
#25 VIOLENCE TRAIL
#26 SAVAGE DAWN
#27 DEATH DRIVE
#28 EVE OF EVIL
#29 THE LIVING, THE DYING AND THE DEAD
#30 TOWERING NIGHTMARE
#31 THE GUILTY ONES

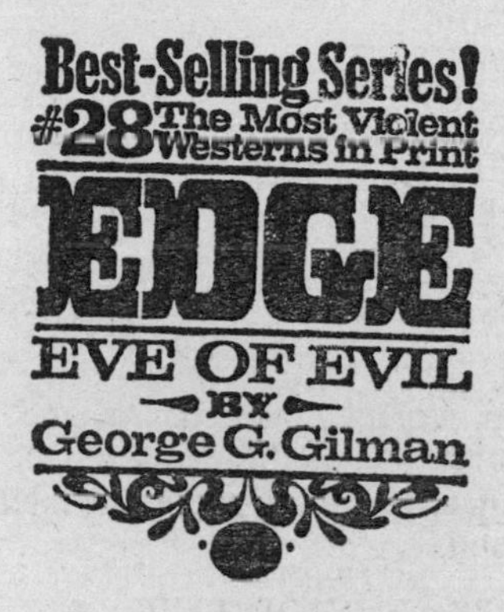

PINNACLE BOOKS LOS ANGELES

This is a work of fiction. All the characters and events portrayed in this book are fictional, and any resemblance to real people or incidents is purely coincidental.

EDGE #28: EVE OF EVIL

First American edition.
First published in Great Britain by
New English Library, September 1978

A Pinnacle Books edition, published by special arrangement with New English Library, London.
First printing, November 1978
Second printing, November 1979

ISBN: 0-523-40204-X

Cover illustration by Bruce Minney

Printed in the United States of America

PINNACLE BOOKS, INC.
2029 Century Park East
Los Angeles, California 90067

for:

J. C.
who had a drink or two
in my favorite saloon

EVE OF EVIL

Chapter One

THE man called Edge eased open the door of the Three Horseshoes Saloon and looked out from the almost-pitch darkness at a world of bright color. White and green and yellow and blue. He blinked just once against the dazzle of sunrise across the snow-covered mountainscape, then pulled the door fully open and stretched his arms as he arched his back. These actions dispelled the final remnants of sleep from his brain and muscles. The biting chill of the outside air had no effect, for it could not have been more than a degree colder than the atmosphere inside.

For long moments his narrowed eyes shifted from left and right and back again, surveying the distant wilderness and the closer evidence of civilization's comings and goings. Then he worked saliva into his mouth, swilled it around with his tongue, and spat it out in a long stream to mar the perfect whiteness of the night's snowfall. His expression revealed nothing of what he felt—whether he had tried to rid himself of the aftertaste of yesterday's cigarettes or had registered a tacit comment on the view his eyes had so carefully studied.

He turned and went back into the depths of the saloon, leaving the door open so that the bleak sunlight could penetrate. The brightness emphasized the squalor of the setting and the conformity of the man's appearance with his surroundings. For the saloon was cold and neglected and had been empty of all signs of life for a very long time before Edge sought its shelter from the previous night's blizzard.

It was a square, high-ceilinged room with a bar counter stretching almost the whole length of the rear wall. There were no longer any bottles and glasses on the shelf in back of the counter. Nor were there any tables and chairs in front of it. A single music stand stood on a small platform, like a soot-blackened skeleton. Rusted hooks on the walls showed where lamps had once hung. The pot-bellied stove remained bolted to the floor in the center of the saloon but its smoke stack was gone. The hole this had left in the roof had been boarded up. Like the two windows facing the street. The big one-piece door that supplemented the batwings had also been securely fastened until Edge had levered off the barring plank with the barrel of his Winchester.

It had been abandoned and left empty of all that had once given it life and character. But secured against all but the most determined intruder—perhaps in the hope that one day it would re-open and become re-established for its original purpose.

But the decay of neglect had made such a hope falser with each day that elapsed. Termites and damp had attacked the timbers of the walls. And rats had chewed up through the flooring to forage for whatever scraps of food had been left in the wake of the long ago departure. And the outside fabric of the building had been ravaged by the worst weapons the high country Wyoming climate could command. So that the place was dank with the rancid odor of perpetual damp and constantly chilled by drafts through countless cracks and holes, which nobody had been on hand to plug.

The fire that the man started in the stackless stove offered little warmth to ease the discomfort of the cold.

But it provided sufficient heat to simmer and then boil a pot of water liberally laced with coffee grounds.

To avoid the smoke, which issued from the stove to fill the saloon and mask the smell of damp rottenness, Edge moved again to the door and peered out across the mountainscape spread south from the decaying ghost town, which had been his refuge from the night's storm.

He was a tall, lean, solidly built man—three inches above six feet and weighing close to two hundred pounds: the flesh hardpacked and evenly distributed over his frame. His features and their coloring marked him as a man with a dual nationality heritage—drawn in fact from a Mexican father and a Scandinavian mother. It was a lean but not a thin face with high cheekbones beneath permanently narrowed eyes under heavily hooded lids. The pupils of the eyes were of the lightest blue and when they lacked expression—which was for most of the time—this coloration gave them the look of ice slivers caught by the first rays of the morning sun.

Between the cheekbones and the firm jawline the skin was pulled taut, flanking a hawklike nose and a wide, thin-lipped mouth. The skin was darkened by his Mexican bloodline, this natural pigmentation shaded still more by exposure to the extremes of weather. And deeply scored by countless lines cut into its every surface. The aging process to his late thirties had inscribed some of these lines. Burning sun and biting winds had also contributed. But many more—the deepest that spread from the corners of his eyes and mouth—were obviously the physical marks of mental suffering, less subtle than the scar tissue of old bullet wounds on his body, but in their own way just as readable. Especially when seen as an intrinsic part of the whole: giving reason for the coldness of the slitted blue eyes and the latent cruelty in the set of the lips.

Even though the face bathed by early morning sunlight was unwashed and unshaven—a thickening of the bristles along the top lip and to either side of the mouth indicating a sparse moustache—there was, nevertheless, an indication of handsomeness about the features. But this was contradicted by the slightest movement of the head, which at once transformed the face into a mask of ugliness. Thus it was that Edge's countenance, framed by jet black hair that fell to a length so that it brushed his shoulders, could be viewed as either handsome or ugly: the opinion formed entirely within the mind of the beholder.

His clothing was as unkempt as the man it fitted. A black, low-crowned, wide-brimmed Stetson. A gray shirt and a kerchief of the same color, loosely knotted so that it did not quite conceal the dully colored beads that he wore around his throat on a leather thong. Black denim pants with the cuffs worn outside spurless riding boots. Around his waist there was a gunbelt with a shell in every loop, a holster hanging from the right side and tied down to his thigh, housing a Remington revolver. Caped over his shoulders—not yet properly worn after serving as an additional blanket while he slept—was a thick, knee-length jacket of black leather.

All the clothing was stained, rumpled and torn, ill-used, and long past its prime. Like the saddle and unfurled bedroll in the corner of the saloon behind him, which had been free of most of the night's drafts.

When he backtracked to the stove, claimed the coffee pot, urinated on the flames to extinguish them, and took a mug from his pile of gear, his skin and clothing were stained darker and made to smell staler by the smoke. And, after he had returned to the doorway, poured a mug of coffee and begun to sip the strong brew, he was fleetingly and vaguely aware that he and his immediate surroundings were even more starkly contrasted with the purity of the panorama he looked at. The white of the snow, the green of the firs, the blue of the sky, and the yellow of the sun. All of this clean and unsullied. Component parts of a new born day in the Wind River range of mountains. Mint new and innocently awaiting the outcome of a man's intrusion.

Edge drank his coffee and gave no further consideration to the image of himself as a crude invader upon a chaste landscape, for it was not in his nature to waste time with contemplation of the abstracts of life. Last night's snowstorm had forced him to find shelter and Providence had supplied the abandoned buildings of a ghost town. This morning, his bleak-eyed surveys of the broad valley stretching to the south were not concerned with the unproductive appreciation of natural beauty. Rather, he was checking the terrain for signs that other men were close by. And planning the easiest route away from the town and saloon that had served a purpose.

He had been heading northwest across the Continental Divide when the dark clouds delivered on their day-long threat and began to shed their snow. But, as was so often the case with the man named Edge, there had been no specific destination in mind. The future had been in the hands of his destiny, more uncertain perhaps than that of any other man. The present he controlled more tightly than most. Like all, the past was a memory with—freshest in his mind—the cattle drive from south Texas to Laramie and the lone ride across the high plains and up into the mountains.

Thus, as he finished the second mug of coffee, it was of no consequence to him that the terrain of the Wind River range suggested that his new course lay south. For he was as likely to have a new experience with evil in this direction as in any other.

Then, just as he was about to empty the coffee

grounds from the pot on to the snow marked only by spittle, he saw the two riders. And immediately breathed a low sigh of resignation to expect the worst.

They were heading for the ghost town from the southwest, coming down the slope of the valley side with a brand of slow-paced relentlessness, sure of their ground as they steered their mounts along a curving course through knee-deep snow. Following a known trail, Edge guessed. Which offered him the possibility of an alternative way out of the valley.

He watched them from the ridge to a clump of timber, then withdrew into the saloon, which was still tainted with old smoke. He emptied the contents of the coffee pot onto the already dead ashes in the stove and then continued his preparations to leave by rolling up his bedding and taking it and his saddle over to the door. The saddle was so placed that the stock of the booted Winchester jutted upward. And, after he had donned the leather coat he did not fasten the buttons. This allowed him easy access to the butt of the holstered Remington low on his right side.

Then he looked outside again, but with more caution now, taking trouble to see without being seen.

The tracks left by the mounts of the men emerged from the stand of firs and inscribed another curve through the snow, this time in the opposite direction. They went from sight behind a rearing outcrop of rock, swinging away from the town. But, when the men reappeared it was to make a right-angle turn at the end of the outcrop and head in a straight line up the gentle slope toward the spot where Edge waited.

The Mexican-Scandinavian half-breed released the catches on the batwings and the half doors swung across the saloon entrance. Then he stepped back and to the side, into the shadows not yet penetrated by the shafting sunlight from the southeast. He adjusted the saddle into the angle of wall and floor so that the stock of the booted rifle was even more accessible to his left hand.

Not that there was anything in the appearance or demeanor of the approaching men to indicate they were intent upon making trouble. One was six feet tall, the other a head shorter. They were suitably dressed for winter in the mountains. Stetson hats with scarves wrapped around their heads to protect their ears and jaws from the cold. Snow goggles to diminish the glare to their eyes. Fur jackets cut to mid-calf length. Sheepskin chaps supplementing their pants. They rode big, strong-looking stallions saddled Western-style and laden with the gear and accouterments of cowhands. Line riders, maybe. There was a rifle in each boot. With the goggles and wrap-around scarves concealing so much of their faces the men may have appeared a little menacing to anyone with a nervous disposition. Edge was not nervous. Merely cautious. For he had survived for the greater part of his life by assuming that every stranger was a deadly enemy until events proved otherwise.

The trail the riders knew to be beneath the two-foot-deep layer of crisp snow turned them away from the Three Horseshoes Saloon and brought them into town midway along the only street. This took them out of sight of Edge again. But he could hear them after awhile—the muted crunching of snow being compacted under hooves and the creak of ungreased harness leather.

As these sounds grew louder, the riders moving west along the street, Edge moved closer to the batwings and raised his right hand to drape it over the butt of the holstered Remington.

Then the horses were reined to a halt.

"Store'll be as good a place as any, Ben?" one of them suggested, a subservient inflection adding the query.

"Why not?" the other replied, disgruntled.

They dismounted in front of the building next door to the saloon. There was a flapping sound as one of the men beat his arms to his chest, seeking warmth from exercise.

"Put the horses in the stable out back of the saloon, Ben?"

The half-breed tightened his grip around the butt of the Remington, curling a finger to the trigger and resting a thumb to the hammer. His own black gelding was cold and hungry in the saloon's livery.

"The hell with that, Wes!" Ben growled. "Hitch 'em out here. We left sign can be seen from miles away."

"Guess you're right."

"Ain't I always? Open up the door, Wes."

Booted feet crunched snow, then there was the tortured sound of rusted nails being wrenched from timber as the board across the store door was levered free. After Ben and Wes had creaked open the door and stepped across the threshold, cold and empty silence became re-established in the ghost town.

The silence half lied, of course. Bitterly cold it certainly was, the bright sunlight emphasizing the lack of warmth. But hidden just beneath the pretense were the tiny sounds of living things—the breathing and the heartbeats of three men and three horses.

Edge leaned forward to look out over the batwings and along the street. During the night blizzard that had forced him to seek shelter he had received only a fleeting impression of the town, its buildings seen only as blurred shadows through the slanting, wind-driven flakes.

Now he saw them with stark clarity: ugly man-made and man-abandoned scars on the beautiful, snow-whitened body of the mountainside.

The saloon stood in a sort of aloof isolation on the north side of the street's western end. Across a vacant lot was the store with the stallions hitched outside and the men inside. Beyond this were other business premises—a bank, a stage depot, a barber shop, another store, and a law office. Across from these was a row of houses with, at the far end, a small church.

All the buildings were of single-story-frame construction, abandoned and dilapidated. The blizzard had piled snow into deep drifts against rotting and warped north facing walls. Two sets of tracks in the snow marked the route of Ben and Wes from between two houses, along the street, and up to the front of the store.

A broader pattern of disturbed snow started to show on the southeast slope of the valley, following precisely the same route Edge had taken to reach the town. This new ugliness on nature's post-blizzard beauty was caused by a roofed buggy with a single horse in the shafts—as yet over a mile distant from town.

With a low grunt of mild dissatisfaction, Edge withdrew his head into cover and stepped to the other side of the saloon entrance. And pulled his hat brim low down to shade his eyes from the direct glare of the unwarm sun, which hung above the ridge behind the approaching buggy.

Then he became infinitely patient again: resigned to, rather than content with, the decree of his ruling fate, which had caused him to be in this place at this time. Certain of only one thing—that he would not make the first move to involve himself in whatever was about to happen here.

". . . still say we should've stayed inside, Ben!" Wes complained above the crunching of snow beneath their feet.

Ben spat forcefully. "They seen our sign," he countered with a sigh. "They seen our horses. They know there ain't no way they can get away from us in that rig. And they got no reason to expect we're gonna—"

"All right, all right!" Wes surrendered morosely. "You know what you're doin'."

"Don't I always?"

They had come to a halt at the center of the street, their backs toward the saloon as they gazed across the narrowing distance between town and the buggy. The only difference in their appearance since Edge had last seen them was that they had unfastened the buttons of their long coats.

"This is a hell of a thin' to have to do, Ben."

"Ain't it though." The taller man's tone was sardonic in contrast to Wes's deep-seated anxiety.

"Miss Lassiter and me used to get on real fine. Used to call me Uncle Wesley. You remember that?"

"Yeah, I remember," Ben confirmed, his own self-confidence beginning to wane. "You want a belt?"

"Sure."

"Here you are. Take a belt and then keep your mouth buttoned!"

His voice was harsh as he worked to mask his true feelings. In the crystal clear purity of the mountain air Edge could hear the glug of liquor passing down Wes's throat.

"That's enough, damn it!" Ben snarled, and snatched back the bottle just as Edge chanced a brief look toward the two men.

"I—"

"And I told you to button it!" Ben cut in. He took a gulp from the bottle himself before capping it and thrusting it into a deep pocket of his long coat.

The progress of the buggy could be heard then—compacting snow beneath hooves and wheelrims and the creaking of springs and timber.

"Jesus, do I want to crap," Wes rasped.

"Think of somethin' else, damn it!" his partner commanded.

"Uncle Wesley? Is that you, Uncle Wesley?"

The girl's voice was shrill—whether with the excitement of pleasure or nervousness it was impossible to tell.

"Yeah, Miss Lassiter, it's me all right."

Wes's tone was thick, as if the words had to be forced through something wet and sticky blocking his throat.

"And Ben? Ben Buel?"

The taller man waited until the buggy had been brought to a halt before he replied: "Right again, miss. And the guy with you is the one you wrote your pa about?"

When he had first seen it in the white distance, Edge had been unable to tell how many people had been aboard the buggy. Now he leaned forward to chance another look diagonally along the street.

The cut-under buggy had been halted with the dappled gray gelding twenty feet in front of Ben Buel and Wes. On the padded seat in the cold shade of the roof was a young couple in their early twenties. They were encased in thick coats buttoned to the throat and with the collars turned up. A heavy blanket draped their knees. From his brief glimpse of them, Edge got an impression of a soon-to-be beautiful blonde-haired girl and a young man with the handsome features and shaded coloration of a Mexican. The girl had been happy to see old friends but this emotion was just beginning to be replaced by another. Her companion looked as if the expression of fear had been frozen on to his face by the first frost of the Wyoming winter.

"Yes, this is Joe. Joe Redeker. I'm real glad Dad got my letter and sent you out to meet us. What with the snow I guess it's not easy to reach home. I've been telling Joe all about the place and he's real anxious to see it. He'll be a great help—"

"Forget it, Maria," Joe interrupted the too-fast, too-shrill gushing words of the girl. "Seems I've got somethin' else to be real anxious about now."

His voice belied his looks, not accented, sounding the same midwestern drawl as when Edge talked.

"We're actin' on your pa's orders, miss," Buel said quickly as Maria Lassiter vented a sound between a gasp and a scream. "He said for us to kill your beau."

"And you know us hands have to do everythin' the boss says," Wes pleaded.

"Button it, for Chrissakes!" Buel used anger to mask his true feelings again. "Go help her down and take her inside the store. She don't have to watch this."

"Sure, Ben!"

Wes was eager, grasping the opportunity to be away from the center of the scene when the murder took place.

Edge peered outside again: watching for longer than before. The shorter Wes had already crunched snow as far as the side of the horse and was extending his hands in preparation to assist the girl down from the buggy. But she made no move to cooperate—rather, she was pressing herself hard against the back of the padded seat. Her posture emphasized the pregnant hump contoured by the shared blanket.

At her side, the freezing effect of fear was transmitted from Redeker's dark brown face to his body and limbs. He sat like a waxen figure, the reins still firmly clenched in his gloved hands. Then his eyes began to move, switching from one side of the sockets to the other to apportion the reason for his fear equally between the goggled men.

"Ain't nothin' personal, kid," Buel offered coldly, controlling his reluctance and mouthing the excuse simply to fill the hard, taut silence. "But the boss is mighty angry that you—"

"No!" the girl exploded, and snatched her right hand out from under the blanket. Then, in a further flurry of movement, she leaned forward—out of the shade of the buggy's roof. Like Redeker, she wore gloves. Of thin buckskin that did not hamper her actions as she cocked the hammer of a Frontier Colt and curled a finger to the trigger.

Wes froze in his arms-extended attitude. Ben Buel grunted and drew a revolver that was a match for the one in the girl's hand.

But her gun did not threaten either man. Instead, she raised it to her head and pressed the muzzle tight to her right temple.

"Sonofabitch!" Buel snarled.

"What'll we do, Ben?" Wes croaked.

Redeker was able to move. To turn his head and see the cause of the men's dismay. His own fear deepened. "Maria!" he cried.

Edge continued to watch the center-street tableau with glinting-eyed coldness, feeling not the slightest inclination to break the stalemate that existed. If he experienced anything at all it was merely a mild irritation with the quartet out in the snow—that through no fault of their own they were delaying his departure from the ghost town.

"Let them explain my death as well as yours, Joe!" the girl said shrilly. "Without you, I don't want to live. And the baby—"

"Don't be a fool, Miss Lassiter!" Buel cut in. A note of desperation crept into his voice. "Your pa told us he's ready to forgive and forget what you done. Hell, he might even let you keep the kid."

His Colt maintained a rock-steady aim on Redeker, as certain of its target as was the similar gun in the girl's hand.

"Put up your gun and the both of you mount your horses and go back to the ranch," Maria Lassiter instructed. She had come up from the depthless chasm of terror and had a tight grip of ice-cold composure. Her mind was made up and was closed to everything except the decision she had made. "Joe will take me someplace else to have my baby. My father need never know of this meeting. Or . . . he'll know you stood by and allowed me to blow out my brains."

"Sure, Ben!" Wes said eagerly after stretched seconds of heavy silence. "We can hang around awhile. Then head back. The boss don't have to know—"

"Will he agree, too?" Joe Redeker asked. Hopelessly.

As Wes began to voice his enthusiastic agreement with the girl's plan, Redeker had shifted his eyes from the taller to the shorter man. But he was distracted by something on the periphery of his vision. And did a double-take to find his gaze trapped by the glinting slivers of the half-breed's impassive eyes.

The girl looked in the direction of the boy's nod and just for an instant the sight of Edge's sunlit head and shoulders above the tops of the batwings threatened a tremour of nervousness that could have tightened her finger against the trigger.

But the movements of others trapped her into immobility inside a capsule of horrified fascination.

The two men on the ground snapped their heads around to show their inhumanlike goggled faces to Edge.

"Who . . . ?" Wes croaked.

"Sonofabitch!" his partner added, kicking his right foot against the snow to power a turn of his body. His arm and gun hand swung at a greater speed. "Get him!"

Wes continued to be slower in his reactions. Actually had to claw twice before his right hand fastened on the butt of his revolver and drew it from the holster.

Edge could have stepped back into the cover of the saloon. There to shout his intention of not mixing in on other people's business. But the intention so blatantly displayed on Ben Buel's half-concealed face caused the half-breed to instantly reject retreat. Buel meant to kill him, had compounded the sin by calling upon Wes to abet him. The intention was a reflex to instinct, triggered by the desire to survive against an unexpected danger. Which might have been regretted and forgotten had Edge backed off and used his voice.

But Edge saw only the pulled-back lips and snarling teeth of the present. Then the blank hole of the Colt muzzle. And responded instinctively to the present threat without further attempt to project events into the future.

So he stepped forward, his right knee pushing open one of the batwing doors. The Remington came clear of his holster with the hammer cocked. And he squeezed the trigger the instant the gun was leveled at its target.

Buel took the bullet in the chest, left of center. His teeth sprang apart to give vent to a growl of dismay. Blood oozed from the bullethole in his coat and blossomed into an enlarging stain. As his right arm sagged and his fingers released their hold on the Colt, he tried to stagger backward. But the snow was too deep and his legs did not have the strength to drag themselves through it. He sat down hard on his rump. His teeth clenched tightly together again.

"Sonofabitch," he said in a tone of surprise. And died, his body and head flopping forward. The rapidly receding heat of his corpse melted a little snow and his folded-over form sank an inch or so before it became totally inert.

Edge heard the final word of the dying man but did

not watch the death. As soon as the gun had fallen from Buel's grasp, the half-breed directed his unblinking eyes and his freshly cocked Remington toward Wes.

The shorter of the Lassiter hands was in the grip of a paroxysm of shaking. But he still held on to his Colt and Buel's dying curse caused a more violent shudder that squeezed his finger against the trigger. The bullet hissed a hole through the snow ten feet away from Wes's toecaps.

A third shot sounded like an instantaneous echo of the second. And Wes vomited a great splash of spittle-run blood across the snow. Then he coughed and the damaging bullet rolled over his lower lip and became lodged in the knot of the scarf tied under his chin. The cough was powered by Wes's final breath and he crumpled limply into death, not quite covering the scarlet mess he had made on the snow. There was very little blood around the small hole in the hairless nape of his neck.

It was Joe Redeker who had fired the killing shot, having snatched the Colt from the unresponsive girl while she was still spellbound by the horror of seeing Buel die.

"Don't, feller," Edge urged softly as he stepped through the batwings on to the snow.

"What?" the boy asked thickly. He looked suddenly very sick.

"Point that gun at me. I kill people who do that. Warn them first, if there's the time."

Redeker looked down at the Colt in his left hand. He was in the process of swinging it to cover the tall, lean man at the saloon entrance. But then he pulled his arm in toward his body and allowed the revolver to drop on to the shared blanket.

"Who are you?" Maria Lassiter asked, enunciating

her words with great care, as if she was unsure of what they would be until she heard them.

"Edge." He touched the brim of his hat.

"Maria and me are indebted to you, Mr. Edge," the boy offered, his voice sounding more normal.

The half-breed shook his head as he holstered the Remington. "When it happened it was just between him and me. You benefited. It didn't cost me anything."

"When I asked who you were, I didn't just mean your name." Like Redeker, she was making a fast recovery from shock.

The boy took her hand and held on to it tightly. She allowed him to do this, seemingly because she was unaware of the contact. Her brown eyes, which offered the strongest promise of beauty to come, remained firmly focussed upon the bristled features of the half-breed.

"Leave it, Maria. Let's just thank our lucky stars he was here." Redeker shifted his intent gaze from the ardently interested expression of the girl to the totally dispassionate face of Edge. "No matter what you say, mister, we're beholden to you."

The half-breed acknowledged this with a nod.

"You don't know my father?" Maria Lassiter asked, reluctant to do as Redeker had suggested.

"No."

"Nor Buel or Wesley Young?" She was prepared for another negative response and was already set to disbelieve it.

"That's right."

"Then why?" she demanded. "Why did you kill Buel? And you'd have shot Uncle . . . Young if Joe hadn't done it."

She didn't like what she was saying—was afraid of the implications. Her youthful face expressed a keen desire to be given an explanation she could both understand and approve of.

Redeker was afraid again, fearful the undemonstrative half-breed would read the accusation in the girl's words and respond to it with renewed violence.

Edge pursed his lips and rasped the back of a hand over his bristled jaw. "I'd have to think about that," he said evenly.

"You mean you don't know why?" the girl gasped, as the half-breed turned his back on the couple in the buggy and the corpses crumpled in the snow.

Edge halted on the threshold of the saloon, holding open the batwing doors with both hands. There was the suggestion of a smile at the upturned corners of his mouth, but the cold glitter of his eyes contradicted this. "I said I'd have to think about it," he reiterated and his tone confirmed neither the humor of the set of his mouth nor the harshness of his eyes. "And I always think best when it's quiet." He lowered his eyes just a fraction to direct their gaze at the distended belly of Maria Lassiter contoured by the blanket. "So maybe we should have what they call a pregnant pause?"

Chapter Two

EDGE could hear them talking in low, tense tones as he hefted his gear up from the floor of the saloon, the saddle over his right shoulder and the bedroll under his left arm. When he stepped outside again they curtailed the talk and abruptly—guiltily—shifted their gazes away from the doorway, and found themselves staring fearfully at the stiffening corpses in the snow.

Then returned to their discussion bordering on argument as he moved along the side of the saloon toward the stable at the rear. The sense of what they were saying to each other did not carry to the half-breed, but it was apparent that the short, lean, muscular Redeker was trying to dissuade the pregnant girl from doing something she was determined to achieve.

Inside the stable, with the bulk of the store between himself and the young couple, he could hear nothing except the small sounds he made in saddling the black gelding and lashing on the bedroll. The horse eyed him dispiritedly in equine disapproval that the man had brought no feed.

"It's a tough world all over," Edge murmured, stroking the animal's neck before leading him outside and along the alley to the street.

The secretive exchange had been completed and the boy had won the verbal contest. He expressed mild satisfaction while Maria suffered defeat with tight-lipped sullenness.

Nobody said anything until after the half-breed had unhitched the reins of the dead men's stallions from the rail in front of the store. Then, as he mounted his gelding, Redeker called, "Mr. Edge?"

"Yeah?"

"Me and Maria are gonna get outta this part of the country just as fast as we can."

"Best it should be to where there's a doctor, kid," the half-breed advised, and again looked pointedly at the blanket-contoured hump of the girl's belly. The Colt was no longer in sight. Maria glanced fleetingly at him and her big brown eyes explicitly expressed a wish he was also gone.

Redeker nodded shortly. "There should be another two weeks before the baby comes. But we aim to make Fallon long before then. By nightfall if we're lucky. Maria says they got a doctor there."

"That's fine." He tugged gently on the reins to head the gelding west.

The boy hurried on, leaning forward from the buggy seat to peer along the street in Edge's chosen direction. "Like I told you, we're beholden to you."

"Once would have been enough, kid."

"Listen to him, why don't you!" the girl snapped angrily.

Redeker laid a restraining hand on her forearm. But he did not look at her, his dark, anxious eyes fixed upon the half-breed's unresponsive face. "Don't think hard of her. It's been a bad start to the day. We come all the way up from Denver hopeful Cole Lassiter would be real pleased to see us. Only to have this happen."

He eyed the bodies of Buel and Young with a brand of bitterness that seemed to threaten tears.

"I just told my horse."

Redeker blinked his confusion, looking very callow.

"It's a tough world all over," Edge amplified.

The boy nodded emphatically. "Around here especially," he warned. "I ain't never met Maria's father. But she's told me a lot about him. None of it good. I never wanted to come. Maria did. She figured that having a grandchild due to arrive any day might change her father for the better."

The girl uttered an unfeminine grunt of impatience. "He doesn't want to hear the story of our lives, Joe!" she chided. And fixed her disapproving eyes on Edge's face. "I don't like you, mister. And although I think I could have handled Wes Young and Ben Buel, Joe has half convinced me that you may have saved his life. What he's trying to do now is convince you it would be better if you didn't ride west from here. Because, if you do go that way, you'll be on Lassiter range for at least two days. In that time my father is likely to find out two of his best hands have been killed. And strangers will be less welcome on the Bar-M spread than they usually are."

"Obliged," Edge acknowledged, and nudged the flanks of the gelding with his heels. The animal started lethargically forward, then was turned to head across the street over the snow already disturbed by the horses of Buel and Young as they entered the town.

He sensed the eyes of the young couple staring at his back. Then heard another burst of low-voiced talk. This time, Maria won her point.

Redeker growled a command and the buggy creaked and rattled into motion, the arched design of the vehicle's body allowing the big front wheels to turn sharply and bring it completely around in its own length.

Just before Edge rode between two houses on the south side of the street and as the buggy began to back track over the rutted sign of its approach, he heard part of a sourly spoken comment:

". . . him, Joseph, on account of he's the kind that goes lookin' for trouble wherever . . ."

The intervening buildings blocked off the rest of the girl's jibe and the lengthening distance drew a complete veil over the sounds of the buggy's progress. After awhile, it would have been possible for Joe and Maria to see Edge and for him to see them. But nobody turned around as the lone rider headed up the southwest trail and the buggy crawled in a southeast direction. For the town, now inhabited by two more ghosts, was behind them; soon, was below them as they headed in opposite directions for the ridges flanking the valley.

The couple was riding toward a predetermined destination—the town of Fallon, with its promise of a doctor who would help deliver their baby. Edge was aiming for . . . ?

Maria Lassiter had almost been right, except her harsh tone had accused the half-breed of "lookin' for trouble" with a selfish motive.

Just twice had this been so. Once, when he rode out on a vengeance trail in search of the men who tortured and murdered his kid brother. Then again, many years later, when a conviction that Sioux Indians had taken his wife triggered another bloody journey on which to kill was of more import than to survive.

For the rest of the time?

Before Jamie's terrifying and agonizing death on the Iowa farmstead, the man who was now called Edge had never needed to question his motives. He was Josiah C. Hedges then, the elder son of a tough Mexican father and a beautiful Swedish mother. Life had been hard but uncomplicated by any events that had no direct bearing on eking the necessities of living from the farm on the prairie. Then, after the death of his parents, it had become simpler in many respects.

Until the first shots of the War Between the States portended the end to what once had been.

Whenever he considered the coming of war and his

response to it, the man who now rode up a valley side in the Wind River range never sought to use this interlude in his history to justify what he was. For he acknowledged that countless other boys had been forged into men by the same brutal process, yet had returned in peace to take up the same style of life as before.

So to his mind the decision that he should go to war while Jamie remained at home to tend the farm was not a momentous one. At the time he took it, in consultation with his younger brother, it had seemed the obvious thing to do.

War taught him how to kill and to survive to kill again. And he was an attentive and quick-to-learn pupil during the harshly cruel lessons on the battlefields of the eastern states. For no other reason than he believed in the cause for which he was fighting and was anxious that he should be on the winning side.

He rode for the Union cavalry, first as a lieutenant and then a captain. And had to fight a double war—against the Confederate enemy and against six men under his command. A half dozen of the most amoral and vicious killers who ever donned army uniforms. Thus did he have to hone his wits as well as his military skills in order to survive the enmity of both foe and so-called friends.

And, by the first of many cruel twists of his ruling fate, it was decreed that these six should reach the Iowa farmstead ahead of the discharged Captain Hedges in that euphoric period following the Appomattox peace signing.

Jamie died badly, suffering at the hands of men who regarded mercy as a weakness. But his killers made a fatal error by leaving one of their own dead beside the mutilated corpse of Jamie in front of the burnt-out farm house. Thus was Josiah C. Hedges's first step along the revenge trail given direction.

Was that the most momentous step—most

momentous decision—he took? In retrospect he could consider it so. But at the time there had been no pause for such abstract contemplation. Impulsively, instinctively, recklessly, he had ridden out after the killers. And had found them and made them pay the price for their crime—using his war-taught skills to track them down and to punish them.

During this vengeance hunt, a man who was not perhaps innocent had died by the violent hand of Josiah C. Hedges. But certainly he was innocent of any major crime against his killer and thus had Josiah C. Hedges become wanted for the murder of Elliot Thombs. And, as a result of this and the mispronunciation of his name, had the killer acquired the name of Edge.

His short-lived, tragically ended marriage to Beth had come much later; but there had not been time enough—or Edge had been unwilling—to learn that he was destined never to put down roots nor to form any deep relationship with a fellow human being. There had been examples enough of this between the killing of Jamie and his meeting with Beth, but he had ignored them.

And even after his wife's death—the grief harder to endure than the anguish following Jamie's murder—Edge had striven when the opportunity occurred to carve himself a niche in the peaceful world of ordinary people going about their routine business.

But always the obstacles placed in his path were too difficult to overcome. Always he won only to lose, be it a woman, money, or even a roof over his head. And always there was violence. Blasting gunfire, flashing blades, the screams of the dying, and the crimson gouting of their blood.

Jamie and Beth. A farm in Iowa and another in the Dakotas. As his mind re-spoke the accusing words of Maria Lassiter, these two people and these two places in the distant past were vivid in his memory. He had been to countless other places and known countless other people: some still alive and perhaps just as many as violently dead as his brother and wife.

But, as he achieved the top of the valley side and halted his horse to look back, he purposely elected that they should remain an unknown statistic buried deep in his memory. For he knew that if he gave them close consideration he might discover that the pregnant girl aboard the buggy had spoken the whole truth.

The buggy was only halfway up the opposite slope of the valley, its progress through the snow necessarily slower than that of a horse and rider. The horses of the two dead men, burdened only by saddles and bedrolls, could have traveled much faster. But the pair of stallions were content to trail Edge at the same pace as the gelding.

From the high ground the half-breed had a bird's-eye view of the ghost town with the snow on its single street trampled and littered with two corpses. And it was hard for him, in his present frame of mind, to visualize the same setting with slightly different components had his ruling fate decreed he should have spent the night elsewhere.

He had been down there and he had fired the first shot. They were the actual facts of the incident. Just as he had been in the cantina in the town on the south bank of the Rio Grande where the Taggart father and son had come to hire hands for a cattle drive. The drive that had taken Edge to Laramie at the cost of many lives. And so could be said to be directly responsible for him being in the ghost town at the head of the valley below.

The death of Isabella had triggered events that took him to the Mexican town on the bank of the Rio Grande. . . .

"Shit!" Edge rasped between tightly clenched teeth,

then pursed his lips to direct a stream of saliva at the snow. You're what you goddamn are, is all."

The gelding had pricked his ears to the soft-spoken curse: was expecting the touch of heels to his flanks that moved him forward on to Lassiter range.

Astride him, the rider's face continued to show the silent snarl, which was a sign of a mind troubled by not-to-be-denied doubts. But not for long, because he was not the kind of man to indulge his weaknesses; he had learned from bitter experience that survival depended upon the very opposite of this—the careful nurturing of his strengths.

So, very soon, his lean, lined, dark-hued features resumed their familiar impassive set. The words of Maria Lassiter were forgotten, as were the many memories they had triggered. The self-doubt was still there but it, too, was pushed far into the back of his mind. Irksome only because of the knowledge that it might be re-activated at any time by somebody who cared enough about the man to question his motives.

To the west of the valley the country took the form of a high plain featured with expansive stands of timber and slabs of rock, some towering over a hundred feet high. Snow blanketed everything, softening lines and angles. The crystal clearness of the bitterly cold air emphasized the vast distances to the horizons on every side.

For a long time nothing could be seen to move on the white wilderness except the gelding and its rider and the two stallions. And, after awhile, all signs of Buel's and Young's morning presence on the plain were gone. For their tracks had churned up the snow from the northwest. Edge's route took him southwest. The stallions ignored the sign that indicated the way home and remained on the back tracks of the gelding.

After his period of introspection as he rode up the valley side, the half-breed had taken to constantly surveying his surroundings, his narrowed eyes raking from left to right, his head swinging to direct searching glances back over each shoulder. He would have done this even had Maria Lassiter and Joe Redeker not warned him about the potential dangers of riding across Bar-M range. For it was his nature born of experience to use caution as a weapon: and not only against a specified threat. For his only possession of value was his life and events had proved over and over again that he was in danger of losing this, too—at any moment of the day or night.

And so he rode the snow-covered high plain with fear for company, his dread of dying an ice-cold ball in the pit of his stomach. Dormant for the moment, but primed to explode into life at the first sign of danger. And be controlled by the man and utilized as another weapon: cooling the impulse to recklessness and steadying his physical responses.

So, when he saw the trio of men ahead of him, he was able to form his thin lips into a brief smile of satisfaction. The words of the pregnant girl and the self doubt they had inspired had no lasting effect. His easy, almost involuntary, caution had enabled him to pick out the forms of the men and their horses against the deep shade at the northern fringe of a stand of timber. And the cooling effect of expanding but controlled fear kept his mind open while toning his reflexes. Outwardly, his attitude astride the gelding and the expression on his bristled, cold-pinched face remained casually indifferent to his surroundings.

The timber grew on a gentle slope and the undisturbed layer of snow at the foot of the rise indicated the men had reached their present position by coming down through the trees. They and their mounts were unmoving until the half-breed approached to within fifty feet of passing them. Then, at a single low-voiced word of command, all three spurred their horses out into the virgin snow. To align themselves directly in Edge's path, facing him.

They were dressed in the same manner as the corpses back at the ghost town, but their goggles were pushed up on to their foreheads. The eyes thus revealed were hard and weary, bagged from lack of sleep and dulled by frustrated enmity. They were all of about the same age as Edge, with unshaven faces marked by the scars of lives that had seldom been easy.

"Where do you think you're goin', stranger?" the man who had ordered the blocking move asked hoarsely.

He had the heaviest build inside his bulky clothing.

Edge reined the gelding to a halt some fifteen feet away from them. The stallions stopped twice that distance behind him. The half-breed nodded, indicating the due-west direction beyond the men and horses in his path. "That way."

"No you ain't." This from the shortest of the three. Livid, flesh-twisting scar tissue on the right side of his jaw also made him the ugliest.

All four men sat easy in their saddles, hands holding reins to horns. All had their coats fastened so that holstered revolvers were inaccessible. But rifle stocks jutting from boots were in plain, menacing sight.

"You're trespassin', you know that?" This man had a high-pitched voice, its feminine quality dramatically at odds with his rugged, aggressively hewn features.

"I didn't see no signs," Edge replied evenly.

The top hand of the group nodded. "We ain't fenced the east boundary yet, stranger. That's why we ain't comin' down hard on you. Shortest way off the Bar-M range is south. With this snow you won't reach the barbed wire until sundown, I reckon. Soon as you do, find a gate and go through it. You see any more Bar-M hands, you tell 'em Van Dorn already give you the marchin' orders."

"Hey, Van Dorn!" the man with the scarred jaw growled. "Them horses."

Van Dorn shifted his weary gaze from Edge's unresponsive face toward the riderless stallions. He studied them for a moment, then: "What about them, Raven?"

"The one with the white patch on the shoulder. That looks like Ben Buel's mount."

Van Dorn looked longer and harder at the stallions, screwing up his tired eyes to combat the glare of sun on snow. Then regarded Edge with the same brand of rising suspicion. "What about that, stranger?"

"I wouldn't know, feller."

"Starr," Van Dorn croaked.

"Yes, sir!"

"Go check the brands on them horses."

The man with the high-pitched voice spurred his mount forward through the deep snow. Then decided he distrusted the half-breed's easy attitude and jerked on the reins to command a curving approach to the stallions, taking him wide of the man astride the gelding.

"How come they're trailin' you, stranger?" Van Dorn wanted to know.

Edge had ignored Starr to concentrate on the two men still facing him. They were perturbed by his apparently nonchalant and yet careful study of them. And were no longer confident enough to be relaxed themselves. They sat rigidly straight in their saddles and their gloved hands made small movements over the horns.

"Maybe they like me."

"I goddamn don't!" Raven snarled, anger emphasising the whiteness of the scar tissue on his jaw. "I don't like none of this!"

He shot a glance toward Van Dorn.

"Three to one," the top hand replied and his own voicing of the odds seemed to ease his mind.

The hooves of Starr's mount crunched loudly in the snow. The expelled breath of men and horses made white wisps in the air, like the first signs of gunfire before the sharp reports and stench of exploded powder. Death hovered in the cold, sun bright morning. Waiting for a mistake to be made or a deliberate decision to be taken.

"But ain't no reason for anybody to get—" Van Dorn continued.

To be interrupted by a shrill shout from Starr: "Hey, they both of 'em got the Bar-M brand, damn it!"

Edge had been certain of the outcome of the man's investigation. But could not foretell the reactions of the trio of Lassiter hands. But he had split them up and rattled at least one of them. And was sure that, despite their look of hardness, none was—or would be—a killer by anything except instinct.

All this shaved down the odds a little, by giving him the advantage of speed allied with lethal skill.

He kicked his left foot free of the stirrup and used his right to power a leap from the gelding's back. Both hands released their hold on the reins and horn and gripped the Winchester. He pumped the action even before the barrel was clear of the boot.

Just for a moment, as he fell toward the snow, he considered the jarring possibility that the cushioning whiteness might be a lie: might conceal the crippling hardness of a jagged rock. In such an event, numbing shock or even unconsciousness could prevent him from following through on his first shot. And two men would be left alive.

Then it was as if the world was suddenly blasted into small red pieces by a deafening barrage of awesome gunfire.

His Winchester spat the first, almost insignificant shot, the stock kicking against his shoulder in recoil as the bullet's charge exploded. Then he was down full length in the snow, hardening from its initial softness as it compacted beneath his weight. His target had been Van Dorn, simply because the man's bulk made him easier to hit than Raven.

There was nothing to choose between the speed of the shocked and frightened men as they dragged their own rifles from the boots. Until the bigger man was hit in the chest by the Winchester bullet and released his grip on the gun to clutch at the blood-splashing hole in his coat.

That was when the holocaust and its bedlam of noise broke out.

The first volley of shots tore into the head of Raven. Rifle fire from close range that drilled small holes through one side of his skull and exploded massive, gore-pouring craters on the other.

Edge had time to pump out an expended shell and jack a fresh round into the breech of his rifle and then saw the dying Van Dorn meet his end.

Like the scar-faced man, it was his head that was the target. But his attackers, by accident or design, directed their bullets into his face rather than his skull. There were entry and exit wounds again. But this time whole chunks of crimson flesh were torn free of the bone structure, to fall faster to the snow than the liquid gore.

The half-breed's nightmarish image of the world ending in a bright red explosion was the aberration of just part of a second. Then cold reality was re-established in his mind. And he took the calculated decision to seek out Starr rather than to check on the next move of the deadly newcomers.

He rolled over on to his back, shifting his narrow-eyed gaze and the muzzle of the cocked Winchester away from the limp forms of Van Dorn and Raven tumbling from their snorting mounts. The roll continued, to bring him over on to his left side.

"He's ours, if you don't mind, son!"

Edge already had the shrill-voiced Lassiter hand in the sights of the Winchester. But stayed his finger against the trigger at first pressure. For Starr was not a threat. The man had drawn his rifle from the boot, but then hurled it down into the snow. His arms were thrust high into the air, as if he were trying to grasp the morning sun suspended above his head. His face wore a deep set expression of painful terror, which took on an eerie quality from the big, sightless eyes of the goggle lenses held to his forehead.

"It doesn't have to be over my dead body, feller," the half-breed growled.

"Please don't!" Starr begged, and stood erect in his stirrups to lengthen his reach for the sun and emphasise his surrender. "We was just doin' what the boss told us when we killed them sheep of yours! There weren't nothin' else we could do! Look, I'm givin' up!"

Tears spilled from his small, real eyes. Saliva ran out of a corner of his mouth and made white bubbles in his bristles.

"Yeah, you're givin' up, Starr! The ghost!"

They shot him then. Three men in sheepskin coats with the collars turned up to brush the undersides of their hat brims. Standing knee deep in snow under the trees. With Winchesters to their shoulders.

Just for an instant the sun glinting on the barrels of the rifles was dimmed by muzzle flashes. Starr's scream sounded simultaneously with the single report of the volley. Edge looked toward him and saw the riflemen had taken no chances over the longer range. They had aimed for the larger target of the victim's body, and scored hits in the chest. The impact of the bullets against his flesh forced him to sit down hard in the saddle. Then tipped him backward over the rump of his horse. The animal snorted and pawed at the snow.

Then became calm as the two riderless stallions nearby.

Edge had eased up into a sitting position and he pushed the hammer of his rifle gently to the rest as he swung his hooded eyes away from the new corpse to look again at the men under the trees.

"Merry Christmas to you, son," one of the aging men said wearily as they all lowered their rifles.

"Though it don't look like there's much goodwill about this season," the man on his left muttered.

The third one cleared his throat as he watched the half-breed get to his feet. "Not with three dead men out here and the carcasses of more than a hundred head of our sheep piled in the timber."

He looked about to spill a different brand of tears than those Starr had shed.

"It's Christmas?" Edge asked.

All three were briefly surprised by his ignorance.

"Tomorrow it will be, son. You must have been away from civilization a long time, I reckon."

The half-breed nodded absently. Then asked: "And you're sheepmen?"

"We was until the bastard killed our animals," the one close to tears supplied, not interested in anything outside of his own misery.

But the other two were intrigued by Edge's pensive frown as he ploughed through the snow to his gelding and thrust the rifle back into its boot.

"You got somethin' on your mind goes deeper than these killins, son?"

The half-breed rasped the back of a hand over the bristles on his jaw. "Shepherds," he mused, indicating the three men with a hand. Which he then formed into a fist with the thumb extended to point toward the bullet-riddled body humped in the snow behind him. "A Starr in the east."

He lost the interest of another of the sheepmen who

joined his embittered partner in morose contemplation of the closer corpses of Van Dorn and Raven.

"You don't look like no religious nut, son," the oldest and most garrulous man growled.

"No," Edge murmured absently. "And I guess Joe screwed Maria pregnant."

"Hell, son, you talkin' about the second comin'?"

The half-breed pursed his lips and allowed a brief sigh to escape. Then formed his mouthline into a sardonic smile. "I wouldn't know, feller. They never told me how many times it took them."

Chapter Three

THE flock of sheep, still clad in their unshed winter coats, had been herded into a rope corral deep in the timber, then slaughtered with a barrage of repeater rifle fire. The carnage had been carried out several hours previously, for the carcasses sprawling and piled on the thin carpet of snow under the trees were stiff with *rigor mortis*. The intense cold had suspended decomposition of the flesh but the stench of dried blood in the air was still strong.

The horses of the sheepmen, which were tethered to a low branch, had grown used to the tainted atmosphere. Edge's gelding continued to make nervous sounds and movements until the open air abattoir and its malodorous atmosphere were well behind the departing men.

The half-breed had been invited to ride with the sheepmen back at the scene of human slaughter.

"Name's Owen Craig," the oldest of the trio had introduced. He was pushing sixty with the wrinkled and flaccid facial skin to show it. But his stance was still upright and his movements easy and fluid. His hair was a mixture of jet black and silver gray. His eyes were blue, bright, and alert.

"That there's Doug Smith." This was the man most effected by the loss of the sheep. Perhaps five years Craig's junior. And a bald head shorter than the other's six feet. His flesh had a padding of fat that tended to conceal the wrinkles of the skin. His cheeks bulged beneath his small, bloodshot, dark brown eyes. And his chin took several steps down towards his thick neck.

"I'm Lonny Bassett," the third one volunteered. "And I reckon you ought to stick with us if you wanna get off Lassiter land alive."

He was in the middle, agewise. And also came between the others in his height and build. In fact, he was medium in all things physically visible, except for a bushy gray moustache that looked disproportionately large for his florid face. He had brown eyes, which seemed to show a permanent doleful expression. Like those of a docile animal—a sheep, perhaps.

"Lonny ain't sayin' he don't think you can take care of yourself, son," Craig hastened to add. "We was watchin' you and these here animal killers. And I reckon you could've plugged all three without no help from us."

"Right!" Bassett said quickly, pumping his head up and down to confirm his agreement. "And maybe we should say we're sorry for buttin' in on your play. But it was personal between us and them. After what they done to our animals, we just had to take care of the bastards ourselves."

"Hope you can understand that, son?"

Craig and Bassett were anxiously eager to hear the half-breed's response. Smith was undergoing a gradual change of emotions from grief toward grim satisfaction that a wrong had been righted by resort to revenge.

"No sweat," Edge told the men who were listening. "Just needed them to get out of my way."

"Outta everyone's way now," Craig growled, eyeing the corpses with distaste. Then, to Edge: "Young and Buel, too? Or did you tell this bunch the truth about—"

"The truth, feller." He led his gelding by the reins

into the timber, where the snow was spread more thinly and the animal could muzzle through it to find and crop at sweet grass. "I didn't take notice which was Buel's horse."

The sheepmen followed him, but not the two stallions. They seemed content to stay with their three stablemates from the Bar-M.

"You know what happened to 'em, son?"

Edge was rolling his first cigarette of the day. He lit it, watched eagerly by the older men. "I shot Buel. Feller named Redeker killed Young."

"Hot damn, is Lassiter gonna be mad!" Doug Smith exclaimed in high excitement.

Bassett grinned, showing twin rows of perfectly shaped but darkly stained teeth beneath the big moustache.

"What you got against Cole Lassiter, son?" Craig asked, suddenly burdened by the anxiety he thought all of them should be sharing. "If it ain't buttin' in on personal business, course," he added quickly.

The good humor of Smith and Bassett was abruptly curtailed by their partner's tone. Smith cast nervous glances about him with his bloodshot eyes, and his fleshy cheeks quivered. "You think we maybe oughta be ridin' outta here, Owie?" he suggested. "We been too lucky too long."

Bassett pumped his head in agreement.

Craig vented a non-committal grunt, his deeply interested attention still directed toward Edge. "Unless you got one mighty important reason for ridin' west from here, son, you better not. Best you get off Lassiter range and far away as you can as quick as you can."

"South's best anyway," Bassett encouraged. "On account of there's a regular trail skirting the Bar-M property. That'll take you west faster than across this stinkin' range."

The half-breed looked around at the blue-tinged, eagerly expectant faces of the aging men. And in back of these expressions saw subtle traces of the fear that lurked just beneath the surface exterior.

"Christmas is a bad time for a man to be alone, son," Craig said sadly, his tone implying a conviction that Edge would refuse.

"Let's go."

"You'll go with us?" Bassett blurted.

The half-breed dropped his cigarette stub into the snow and its fire hissed out. "You fellers figure you've been lucky. Maybe it's catching."

His decision drew broad smiles from all three.

"We'll start right now," Craig growled, his excitement almost out of control. "Okay, son?"

"Christmas," Edge replied with a thin-lipped grin.

"How's that, son?" Craig spoke the confusion of all three.

The half-breed lightened his smile. "Present time."

The sheepmen's good-humored peace of mind was short lived and their happiness diminished quickly as they led Edge up the slope through the trees. And, in the small clearing where the sheep had been corralled and slaughtered, each of them hurried to unhitch and mount his horse. They pointedly avoided looking again at the bloodied and stiffened carcasses. And it was obvious that their minds were elsewhere for a long time after the scene of wanton carnage was far behind them: for the set of their lips and look in their eyes provided tacit evidence of bitter hatred directed toward distant enemies, living and dead.

The timber did not finish at the crest of the rise. It rolled over the top and spread down the southern side of the hill, thickening at first then thinning out. The four horses found the going safe and easy, steered over the snow trampled by the flock of sheep and the cowhands who had driven them on their final journey.

It took an hour to ride clear of the wood and in that time a bank of cloud had built up on the northern horizon, dark hued and ominous with the threat of a new blizzard. To the south the white-mantled terrain offered easy riding but promised scant shelter for when the fresh snow fell. For it took the form of rolling hills with shallow inclines and convenient routes around the higher and steeper rises. The sign that marked the route taken by the animals and men toward the timber-covered hill came in from the southwest.

Craig struck out due south across previously untrodden snow. All three sheepmen had difficulty in lighting ready-filled briar pipes as the first breath of a cutting wind curled over the hill behind them to snatch at the match flames. A stronger wind far to the north nudged the cloud bank into motion. Above the quartet of riders, slightly ahead and to the left, the sun shone as brightly and ineffectively as before, innocently unaware of the dirty gray veil that would soon be drawn across its face.

Edge rode beside Craig and Smith and Basset trailed close behind.

"You didn't tell us your name, son."

The dead sheep and the dead men were temporarily forgotten. But there had been no resumption of good humor. The impending storm, the prospect of the long ride ahead, and other factors of which the half-breed had no knowledge weighed heavy on the minds of his companions. And Edge himself discovered he felt uncharacteristically ill at ease without being able to understand why. Knew only that the sensation was not connected with any of the definable reasons that were disturbing the sheepmen.

"Edge," he offered absently.

"Just that, son? No first name?"

"Not any more."

"Good enough, son."

"Has been for a long time."

The elder man looked at the younger with the wisdom of his greater age and then shook his head, perhaps acknowledging that he would never be wise enough to decipher the mystery riding beside him. He drew hard against his pipe, decided he did not like the taste, and knocked the glowing ashes out on to the snow.

"You never did answer that other question, Mr. Edge?"

"Which one was that?"

"One I had no business askin' maybe. About your quarrel with Cole Lassiter and the men that work for him."

"Buel and Young got hexed into pulling guns on me, feller," the half-breed supplied flatly. "Habit of mine to kill folks who do that."

Another habit had command of him now and his narrowed eyes were sweeping the white country for signs of danger, their focus too long to take note of the men riding with him. But he sensed their shocked expressions as they stared at him, convinced by his tone that he had told the truth. But the reason for his callous response to the threat of an aimed gun was too painfully personal to talk about. And it was his secret that, as a young boy, he had pointed a gun at his brother. In play instead of threat. But the motive had made no difference when he squeezed the trigger of the old Sharps rifle, and a bullet that should not have been in the breech had made Jamie a cripple until the day of his agonising death.

"Van Dorn and the others," Edge went on in the same tone. "Figured they were getting ready to pull guns on me."

His explanation and the manner in which he gave it—his expression as dispassionate as his voice—caused the trio of sheepmen to experience a new degree of icy chill that had nothing to do with the strengthening wind and the sudden murkiness of the light as the sun was obscured by cloud.

There was a long period of verbal silence then, while all four men tightened the lanyards of their hats, ensured their coat collars gave the maximum of protection, and looked carefully around to imprint the geography of the terrain on their minds, hopeful of retaining some memory of it when the blinding snow began to drive across their vision.

The clouds raced to blanket the entire blue dome of the sky. The wind at ground level eased to a light, bitterly cold breeze. But everyone knew this was just a lull before the full force of the blizzard hit them.

"But you know his daughter, son?" Craig posed at length.

"Lassiter's?"

"Yeah. She's the Maria you said about awhile ago. The one that's with child."

Edge had been able to calm the strange disturbance in his mind while he attended to the more practical chore of memorizing the directions of prominent features on the landscape that soon would be lost to sight. But the sheepman's mention of the girl's name rekindled the feeling of unease. And with a grunt of irritation he allowed entry to his mind of an explanation he had previously made an effort to bar.

Religion had never, at any high level of consciousness, played an important part in his life. He had been directly concerned with it only as a child when his parents, at irregular intervals, had given unorthodox scripture lessons to the young Josiah and Jamie. Irregular because the work of running the Iowa farm left little time for academic pursuits of any kind. And, for the most part during those formulative years, the godfearing parents had been content that their offspring would learn the virtues of practical Christianity from example.

During the violence of war and the brutal years that followed it, almost every experience of Edge's life had seemed to contribute to a worldly denial of things spiritual.

Until now, as he admitted to himself that he was riding with these three aging men for no other reason than a series of coincidences oddly linked by parallel with the Nativity: that it was Christmas Eve, a girl with the Latin root name of Mary was expecting a child, her man was called Joseph, and Craig and his two partners were sheep herders.

"I guess she's to blame for all this trouble," Craig rasped as Edge gave a slight shake of his head, discounting the presence of a man named Starr from his analogy.

"You can't do that, Owie," Bassett chided. "That kid ain't responsible for what her old man does."

Craig sighed. "Yeah, you're right. But ain't no denyin' it was her gettin' knocked up and headin' for home that drove Cole Lassiter crazy." His voice rose from its vague, pensive level. "That's crazy mad meanin' he become an ornery sonofabitch, son. I ain't sayin' he's gone off his rocker."

"It matter?" Edge asked.

A shrug and then Craig hunched lower into his sheepskin coat as the wind gusted strong for a few moments. "Guess not. Cole Lassiter nor his men never liked us, course. Figures, them runnin' beef and us tendin' sheep. Be a long time yet before cattlemen face up to the fact that they gotta get along with folks like us, I reckon.

"But there weren't no real bad trouble between us until his daughter wrote Lassiter that letter from Denver. Him and his hands just used to cuss us whenever they saw us. And run off our animals whenever they strayed onto Bar-M range."

"Lost us a few the way they done it," Doug Smith snarled. "You gotta be a lot gentler with sheep than with beef."

"Sure," Craig agreed, then had to search his mind to pick up the thread of his interrupted story. "Well, then the letter come. Should have been real private, somethin' like that. But what that letter said was spread around Fallon faster than a quarter horse could run from one end of Main Street to the other. Seemed like everyone down to the smallest kid in the schoolhouse knew Maria was comin' home with a bastard in her womb and bringin' the man that done it with her.

"That was three weeks ago, son. Lonny found out about the letter when he went to town for supplies. They killed three of our animals the next day. Van Dorn and Raven. Cut their throats and dragged them up to our shack behind their horses. Told us the sheep had wandered on to Bar-M range, which I don't doubt they had. Told us that if just one more of our animals stole Bar-M grass they'd slaughter the whole flock. Cole Lassiter's orders. Didn't say nothin' about the letter, course.

"Way I figured it, Lassiter had to unload his feelins someplace. Maria and her beau weren't close enough so he hit out at us on account of we were handy."

"The bastard!" Smith rasped.

"Sure," Craig said, not necessarily in conscious agreement with his fleshy partner. "Couple of days later they started to put up the fence posts and string the barbed wire. But they put it too far south, son. Enclosed open range me and Lonny and Doug had been settled on for almost two years. Didn't own it, course. But Lassiter hadn't never laid claim to it before."

The first flakes of new snow began to slant out of the low, sullen sky and settle on the hats, coats, and horses of the men. Behind them the northern extent of visibility had already closed considerably.

"You put up a fight?" Edge asked, his tone suggesting he had no great interest in the answer.

Craig grimaced as Smith and Bassett took the long cold pipes from between their teeth and pressed them into coat pockets. "Van Dorn showed us papers and he said they proved Lassiter had title to the land. And we couldn't argue with that on account none of us can read. So we just moved our sheep south of the fence line. Grazin' was just as good at the new place.

His expression hardened as the falling snow thickened, the strengthening wind widening the downward angle. "But the bastards didn't give us the time to move our shack. And once the wire was up they said all hell would break loose if we tried to cross it."

The tone of his voice acted to spit out each word like a malevolent missile directed at the man's unseen enemies. "But we shifted that shack, son. A little piece at a time in the nights between when the Bar-M line riders came by. All the inside stuff first so Lassiter hands couldn't see what was happenin'. Then, last night, when it was snowin' so hard a man couldn't see his hand in front of his face, we took off the damn roof, unfixed the walls and hauled all that lumber through the fence. It was one hell of a chore, I can tell you, son."

"You sure you moved it in the right direction, feller?" Edge asked.

"How's that, son?"

The half-breed raised an arm to point ahead and to the right—toward a building in the distance, which was suddenly hidden behind driving snow. "Was hoping that might be home."

"A Bar-M line shack, maybe," Craig supplied morosely. "They're all over the place. Most of them not used any more."

"Lassiter started small and got bigger," Bassett said from behind, having to shout through the sound-blanketing effect of the snow and the whine of its powering wind. "Every time he claimed more land he built a new ring of shacks."

"Figure to use this one," Edge growled, veering his gelding to the right.

Craig's grimace became more deeply etched into the wrinkled flesh of his thin face. "Any port in a storm," he rasped.

"Always found whiskey better when it's this cold," the half-breed murmured. The joke meant only for his own ears, intended to lighten his mood, which was still dictated by the violence-triggered coincidences of this Christmas Eve. The plan did not work.

The driving force of the blizzard struck them harder as they angled southwest across the powerful norther, the snow flakes smashing at the sides of their faces and not melting—clinging to their eyelashes and bristles, which sprouted in flesh as cold as that of corpses.

When they halted their horses in front of the timber-walled, tin-roofed shack they discovered to what extent the icy cold of the blizzard had debilitated them. They had spent too long hunched in their saddles and it was as if their limbs and bodies had been as exposed as their hands and faces to the biting, white-laden wind. It was a slow and painful process to dismount, the aged muscles of the sheepmen protesting more than those of Edge.

It was the half-breed who first made to draw his Winchester from the boot, his narrowed eyes blinking away snowflakes as they raked the blank glass windows and firmly closed door of the shack.

The sheepmen made to follow his example, suddenly effected by the younger man's infectious caution.

"Leave 'em where they be!" a voice shouted. From the right-hand corner of the shack. A man weighed down by a white mantel as heavy as that cloaking the four newcomers stepped into sight. He was sighting along a rifle with the stock plate pressed to his left shoulder.

As all eyes located this man, the door of the shack was wrenched open and a second stepped on to the threshold. There was no snow on his clothing, but it was wet from where the flakes had melted into water and soaked the material. He also aimed a rifle, but from the hip.

"Unless you guys are tired of livin'," the man in the doorway added. "Dead tired, if you know what I mean."

"They know, Al."

"What'll we do, son?" Craig whispered hoarsely.

Edge had his right hand touching the booted Winchester, the palm to the metal of the frame but the fingers not yet started to curl into a clasping fist. He knew it was the physical effect of the harsh weather rather than fear that caused the hand to feel frozen in this useless attitude.

"Give up," he replied evenly. "They got us cold."

Chapter Four

THEY were ordered to step away from the horses with the rifle stocks jutting invitingly from the boots. Then, while the man at the corner of the shack kept them covered, his partner went inside and lit a lamp. The captives were then directed across the threshold by a gesture with the rifle. And, despite the circumstances, all of them entered the shack without reluctance, anxious to escape the driving snow for the false promise of warmth offered by the glow of the kerosene lamp.

When the rifleman who had been outside kicked the door closed behind him, the emptiness of the lamp's bright promise was revealed. The very stillness of the atmosphere inside the shack seemed to emphasise its bitter coldness. And when both Winchesters were aimed at the prisoners from close range, their threat of blasting death and the endless, depthless cold of the grave created a mental sensation to augment the physical.

"Jim Denby and Al Reece," Craig rasped through teeth clenched against the humiliating effect of chattering. "Lassiter hands."

"Figured that much," Edge replied, temporarily disinterested in the two thick-set, middle-thirties men who wore the Bar-M winter trademark of snow goggles pushed up onto their foreheads.

His slitted eyes under the hooded lids, glinting in the lamp light, no longer needed to blink as he surveyed his surroundings. It was a single-room shack, twenty by twenty. Against the rear wall were four bunks, two above two. There was a cold stove near the side wall to the right. Some shelving with closets under them covered the opposite wall. In front of these was a scarred table, leaning drunkenly down on a broken leg. That was all. All bed blankets, provisions, and the other essentials and luxuries for isolated, one-night stopovers had long since been taken away. But the shack had been well built of fine materials and it was still weatherproof even after a protracted period of disuse.

"You done the honors just the one way, sheep-puncher," Denby growled, as the water of melting snow began to drip off his own clothing and that of the prisoners aligned along the front wall of the shack. "Who's your new buddy?"

"Name's Edge," the half-breed supplied, speaking between his hands, which he had raised slowly to his mouth. He blew warm breath into the cupped palms.

"You don't look like no sheep-puncher, Edge."

"And you don't look like you're fixing to kill us right off, feller. So maybe somebody should light a fire in that stove before the weather takes its time with us."

The lamp was of the hurricane type, primarily for use in the open air. It was hung from a hook at the end of one of the higher bunks. Behind the two riflemen. But its light was sufficient for Edge to see the signs of the captors' anxiety. It was easier because of the efforts they were making to conceal their feelings.

"He's got a goddamn nerve, Jim," the shorter and thicker-set Reece sneered.

"And he's also got a point," Denby countered.

"Like the rest of me, damn cold," Edge said through his cupped hands. "You want me to light the fire?"

"Want you to turn around and face the wall, wiseguy," Denby answered, sensing the half-breed's impression of him and hardening his tone and gaze. "Likewise the sheep-punchers. All of you with your hands behind your backs. Anyone tries anythin' stupid the whole lot of you'll go to a real hot place. You know what I mean?"

"Like hell?" Edge said evenly, and did as Denby had instructed.

"That's where all sheepmen are bound." Al Reece growled, and vented a short, harsh laugh as Craig, Bassett, and Smith imitated the half-breed's actions.

"You gonna shoot us in the back?" Bassett asked miserably.

"Could have killed us outside," Edge reminded.

Smith released a long pent up breath in a sigh of relief. "Hey, that's right."

"Just keep hoping all that luck you've been having holds out, feller," the half-breed told him.

Their approach to the line shack had been seen from a distance, giving the Lassiter hands time to prepare for the unwelcome guests. For lengths of rope cut from a lariat were immediately available to tie the prisoners' wrists behind their backs. And a fire was already laid in the stove—required just the striking of a match by Denby to bring it to warm life after the four newcomers had been tied up.

"Turn around now," Denby ordered. "Get their guns, Al."

The two men in command were still ill at ease. And remained so even after Reese had unfastened the prisoners' coats and taken revolvers from the exposed holsters. Three Colts and Edge's Remington. Reece held the surfeit of guns awkwardly, unsure what to do with them. His hands trembled a little.

"Good," Denby said, but his sourly anxious expression suggested he thought things could be much better. "Each of you take a bunk and get on to it. Lay down."

Reece scuttled out of the way as Edge moved and the sheepmen again took their cue from the half-breed. Reece dropped the revolvers heavily to the boarded floor of the shack and reclaimed his Winchester. His jangling nerves even showed in the clumsy way he gripped the rifle.

Edge and Craig took the two lower bunks leaving Bassett and Smith the difficult task of reaching the upper ones without the use of their hands. Reece, on the instructions of the more composed Denby, gave the two men a boost. All four prisoners lay on their sides, their discomfort and disenchantment with the overall situation eased a little by the act of resting in shelter from the storm. And, already, the heat from the recently lit stove had warmed the air and was causing steam to rise from snow-dampened clothing.

"What's this all about, Denby?" Owen Craig asked, trying to inject hardness into his tone and failing dismally.

Now that his prisoners were helpless, Denby's fear was gone. But he continued to be a worried man.

"I don't know, and that's the trouble," he answered. "Only thing I'm sure about is that you sheep-punchers ain't got any right to be on Bar-M range. And I guess you ain't gonna tell me why you are."

"We could beat it outta 'em, Jim!" Reece suggested and now he was feeling better about the situation than his partner, his attitude that of a cowardly bully relishing the prospect of an easy to win triumph. "Maybe kill one of 'em to show we mean business."

Denby eyed his partner with grim-faced distaste. "You wanna do that, Al? Then you wanna tell Mr. Lassiter what you done?"

Outside, the norther howled and whined around the angles of the shack's walls. Snow slanted like a solid mass across the windows, turning mid-day into the depths of night and making the hurricane lamp essential.

"I reckon the boss would be happy to hear it, Jim," Reece said, but his tone lacked force and his bristled face showed an expression revealing the full extent of his doubt.

"Well, you're gonna get the chance, Al," Denby offered, the menace of the words drawing low sounds of alarm from Bassett and Smith. Reece was perplexed for long moments, then became morose as his partner continued, addressing himself to the four men stretched out uncomfortably on the uncovered boards of the bunks. "Me and Al been out fixin' the west boundary fence for more than a week. Which means we're kinda outta touch with what's been happenin'.

"I guess you guys could fill me in. But I ain't about to ask. On account of you'd lie if you've been rubbin' Mr. Lassiter up the wrong way. And I wouldn't believe you if you told me everythin' was hunky-dory between you and the boss."

"So what we gonna do with 'em, Jim?" Reece muttered.

"Keep them here, Al. Soon as this shitty weather stops I'll ride for the big house and tell the boss what we got. You'll stay with them. Be up to you then—if you want to do any beatin' up or killin' before I get back with the real word."

"Sounds like one hell of a waste of time, Jim," Reece growled.

"Time's somethin' we got plenty of, Al."

"Our horses ain't," Edge said flatly. "Unless they get put under cover."

"Do that thing, Al."

"Shit, why me?"

"Because I don't want you to get trigger happy while I'm still around here, that's why," Denby rasped. "Do like you're told, Al."

Reece complied, muttering curses to himself as he went to the door, turning up his coat collar and jamming his hat harder on his head. Wind curled through the momentarily open door, scattering short-lived snowflakes across the floor and belching a billow of black, acrid smoke from under the lid of the stove.

Edge pushed his bound wrists to the right side of his body and rolled on to his back. He scraped the back of his head against the bunk boards to tip the brim of his hat down over his face. His narrowed eyes peered into the self-imposed darkness and he contemplated death, feeling no bitterness that a decision taken without a practical reason had triggered the events that had brought him to the line shack. In his new position on the bunk, the pouched straight razor that he wore from the beaded thong around his neck pressed uncomfortably against the top of his spine: as useless to him now as the Remington on the floor and the Winchester in the boot outside.

"You still won't be able to sleep nights, Denby," Owen Craig accused.

"What's that, sheep-puncher?" the Lassiter hand rasped.

"You know there's a good chance Reece'll kill us all after you're gone. He ain't got all his marbles and he hates sheepmen more than anyone else on the Bar-M."

"Sure I know Al ain't so bright," Denby allowed. "Which is why I can't send him up to the big house. He'll likely take a wrong turn and get to El Paso before he figures it."

"So you'll leave him here to have his crazy fun with us. But you'll be just as much to blame for what happens as him."

"Shuddup, sheep-puncher," Denby ordered harshly, his tone springing from the raw nerve that had been touched. "And all three of you can quit givin' me the evil eye the way you are. Turn over and go to sleep like the big guy, why don't you?"

"Not sleeping, feller," Edge corrected evenly. "Just thinking."

"Best you start to prayin', son," Craig advised. "Makin' your peace with the Almighty before that maniac Reece runs you outta time."

"Maybe the bastard got kicked in the head by a horse and is freezin' to death," Bassett offered miserably from the bunk above where Edge was sprawled.

"That's what's called wishful thinkin', Lonny," Craig growled. "Guess that ain't the kind that our new buddy's doin', right son?"

"Right, feller," the half-breed confirmed. "Was just thinking that this Christmas would have been better with less shepherds and more wise men."

Outside, a woman screamed and a man yelled a curse. The voices seemed to come from a long way off. But all the men in the line shack were familiar with the tricks which falling snow could play with sounds.

"Jesus Christ!" Denby blurted, and swung his rifle to cover the door.

"No, feller," Edge rasped, and moved his head more violently to tip the hat off his face. "That was no heavenly choir."

His glinting gaze found the door just as it was kicked open by a booted foot. And, like the others, he saw just swirling flakes of snow filling the doorway and scattering inside for a stretched second. Then a man materialized, stepping across the threshold to sweep fear-filled eyes over the faces of the men staring at him. A rotund, red-faced, fifty year old man, ill-clothed for the blizzard in the cassock, turned-around collar, and low crowned hat of a priest. His protruding lips quivered and his weak-looking dark eyes seemed on the point of shedding tears as he gasped: "I knew we'd come the wrong way."

"No sweat, father," Edge muttered. "No one ever got killed for making a clerical error."

Chapter Five

HE stumbled further into the shack and almost fell, an ungodly curse ripping from his fat lips. The cause of his near headlong entrance was a woman, shoved hard from behind to crash into him.

"Inside, I told you!" Al Reece snarled. And stepped across the threshold, kicking the door closed as violently as he had opened it.

"Just what in hell is goin' on here?" Denby demanded, shifting his angry and puzzled gaze between his partner and the two unexpected newcomers. "You wanna tell me that, Al?"

The woman still retained something of her former beauty, but living a hard life in tough places had robbed her of more than she had been allowed to keep. She was probably not yet thirty but looked close to being used up. A dyed blonde with brown eyes not quite so dark as the half circles of sagging flesh beneath them. It was in her bone structure that traces of facial beauty still lingered, and also in the regular shape of her nose and the swell without complete fullness of her lips. Her sallow complexion would quickly improve with a few long days in the southern sun.

Despite the ravages time had wrought, she still possessed a striking body vividly shown by the tight-bodiced, low-necklined dress of stained white, which she wore—more unsuited to the weather than the garb of her unlikely companion. The priest looked even shorter than at first, as he stood beside her six-foot-tall, sensually statuesque frame, his head reaching just above the half-exposed semi-orbs of her wet, goose-bumped breasts.

"Caught 'em stealin' grub from our saddlebags, Jim," Reece reported. "What with the wind and all they didn't hear me comin' until I opened the stable doors." He leered. "And I saw them white titties of the broad shinin' up at me like two full moons."

"We weren't stealin', sir!" the priest pleaded, his frightened and watery eyes fixed upon Denby who he had rightly assumed was the dominant partner. "We would have paid. Will still pay. But we were so hungry that it was essential we—"

"He don't mean with money, mister," the woman cut in, and divided her attention between Denby and Reece. Tossing her head to keep the long, yellow hair off her face and turning her body slightly this way and that to give both men a profile and frontal view of her fine breasts. "We don't believe in money."

If she were still suffering from the fear that had triggered her scream, she did not show it. There was confidence based upon long experience of men in the way she spoke and posed for the Lassiter hands. And, in back of this, a trace of honed intelligence in the way she surveyed her surroundings and the other four men while pretending that Reece and Denby commanded her entire attention.

"Daughter is quite right," the priest said quickly, gaining confidence from the woman's attitude and the way in which it had intrigued the Lassiter men.

"You sayin' your daughter is peddlin' her ass for a mess of beef jerky and sourdough bread, mister," Reece demanded incredulously.

"I don't believe it," Bassett whispered hoarsely.

"Precisely, sir," the priest replied eagerly. "Such a

thing does not offend God and therefore how can it offend such a humble servant as I am?"

"Every last one of you, if you're so inclined, gentlemen," the woman offered brightly. And now had the opportunity to look longer and more closely at the quartet lying uncomfortably on the blanketless bunks.

"Obliged, ma'am," Edge responded as the woman's gaze met his and became locked on it for an uncomprehending part of a second. "But we're already in a pretty deep hole."

"Their kind only screw sheep, lady," Reece snapped, the lascivious grin firmly pasted to his bristled face now. "But me, I'm a woman's man first and last. And the last one was a real long time ago. How about this, Jim?"

The grin took on a sick quality, then altered into the lines of a silent but vicious snarl as his partner said:

"It's too easy, Al. It's crazy. I don't trust them."

"Shall I show him, Father?" the woman asked.

"Show them, daughter," the priest agreed.

She took one step away from him and started again to swing her head and body in half turns from the waist to display her blatant sexuality to Denby and Reece. But this time she raised her hands, clawing the fingers toward the palms.

"Never expect a man to make a deal unless he's seen the merchandise out of the wrappin'," she said softly and seductively. The hooks of her fingers fixed over the neckline of her gown at the side of each full breast. Her teeth, perfectly formed and very white gleamed in the lamplight between her tongue moistened lips.

As the priest took off his hat and lowered it in front of his expansive belly, Edge recalled a hot, sun-bright day on the bank of the Rio Grande. Not that stretch where the Mexican village was and where he hired out as a guard to the Big-T herd of Oscar Taggart. But further upstream, in the Big Bend country of Texas.

There had been a woman, a world removed from the one who was the wanton center of attention now. A woman who had meant a lot to him and who could have meant more. Except that she was destined to be lost to him. To leave him as irrecoverably as if death had claimed her.

The woman the priest called daughter wrenched her clawed hands downward. The entire fullness of her breasts were exposed, sagging under the weight of flesh.

Emma Diamond had been totally naked. And had remained unmoving on the hillside.

This woman cupped her breasts and thrust them upward, her fingers moving on the dark brown nipples to distend them.

Emma's shame had been anguished. This woman smiled her triumph of female flesh over the minds of men.

On the Texas hillside, Edge had fired the shot that sent a man to his death with the naked form of a woman his final sight in life.

In the line shack it was the priest who performed this act. Twice.

He shot Jim Denby first, with the reasoning of a skilled gunfighter. For this man, although fascinated by the lewdness of the woman's hands fondling her own flesh, was still suspicious of the newcomers. And his rifle continued to be aimed from the hip.

The gun was in the crown of the priest's hat and the fat little man fired it through the fabric. The bullet tooks its victim in the belly and sent him staggering backward until he hit the wall.

Before the impact of man against timber, the priest had flung his arms wide—the hat in his left hand and the Frontier Colt in his right.

Reece's rifle had been angled down at the floor. He did not even have time to level it before a second gunshot sounded to discharge a bullet into his chest, left of center. There was room for him to take only one step backwards before he hit the door. His heart had made its final beat by then. The strength drained out of him and his booted feet slid in the pool of melted snow beneath them. His legs splayed wide to allow his body to the floor.

"You ain't no priest!" Denby accused bitterly, struggling to bring the rifle to the aim as his energy drained out through the hole in his belly.

"Trained and ordained, sir," came the dispassionate response as the gun hand swung to menace the wounded man. "I doubt if you will go to the place where this can be confirmed."

The Colt bucked in his hand and expelled more acrid smoke into the already tainted atmosphere. It was another heart shot and Denby died with less commotion than his partner. He was already sitting at the angle of floor and wall. He simply tipped forward to fold his body to his legs, the Winchester trapped between.

The woman was as decently dressed as before by then—had simply jerked the bodice of the gown back into place and pushed her breasts into its restraint. Every trace of her recent wantonness had vanished from her face and she now stood submissively beside the priest. Her entire attention was devoted to him while his weak and watery eyes ranged over the men on the bunks.

"I'm right in assuming you will not cause trouble for daughter and I?" he asked.

"We got our hands tied at our backs, son," Owen Craig revealed, his tone of voice a sign of the shock he was still suffering. "But we won't cause none even after you set us free."

The priest pushed his gun back inside his hat and there was a metallic sound as it was clipped into some holding device. Then he put the hat on his head and curled an arm around the narrow waist of the woman.

"Later, perhaps," he said absently as he and she turned toward the door. "For awhile daughter and I must commune with and give thanks to God. This is something we prefer to do in private."

Before they could leave, they had to remove the corpse of Al Reece from the doorway. They stooped to clasp an ankle of the dead man and then dragged him unceremoniously clear of their path. As they went out into the storm, the woman pulling the door closed behind them, the man splayed the fingers of his left hand and moved it forward to grasp the lower curve of her left buttock. The tremor that moved the flesh of her bare shoulders seemed to have little connection with the snowflakes that hit them and melted there.

"Well, I never did!" Doug Smith gasped.

"Figure they have," Edge responded, swinging his feet to the floor and standing up. "Lots of times."

"Denby was right," Craig exclaimed. "This is crazy. And gettin' crazier. They are out there someplace doin' what I think they are, ain't they?"

"Don't give a shit, feller," Edge growled, squatting down beside the old man's bunk. "Just want to be able to do more than just think myself when they get back. There's a razor inside my shirt at the back."

"What?"

"Through my hair and under my collar, feller," Edge said with a note of impatience. "If it's screwing instead of praying they're doing, I don't figure it'll take them long. Just the main event. They went through the preliminaries in here."

Craig had difficulty, working with tied hands behind his back. But he finally managed to draw the razor out from the pouch. Then to hold it firmly while Edge rocked back and forth, running his bonds along the honed-sharp blade. Smith and Bassett looked anxiously down from their upper bunks, the prospect of imminent freedom wrenching their minds away from the weird couple who had provided the opportunity.

"That's a strange place to carry a razor, mister," Smith called down as the rope finally parted and the half-breed stood up.

"You ever think I had it there, feller?" Edge countered as he took the razor and sliced through Craig's bonds.

"How the hell could he?" Bassett defended his partner.

Edge nodded as he rose to free Smith. "Like Denby and Reece and the copulating cleric, feller."

"Oh, it ain't just for shavin'," the man with the too-large moustache gasped as the razor severed the rope around his wrists.

"Bassett's always been a little slow on the uptake," Smith explained, grinning his happiness to be free.

Edge nodded again as he crossed the room to retrieve his Remington. "Takes all sorts to make a world."

The sheepmen picked up their own revolvers and pushed them into the holsters. Then took out the briar pipes and began to tamp aromatic tobacco into the bowls. Edge wiped the mist of condensation off one of the windows and tried to peer out. But he could see no further than the frenetically moving veil of snowflakes that continued to rush out of the sky.

"He wasn't such a bad guy," Owen Craig muttered sadly as the half-breed turned away from the window.

All three men were sitting on the bunk that had been Edge's, hunched forward and sucking the strong smoke of comfort from their pipes. After the initial euphoria of rescue, the overweight Smith and the moustached Bassett seemed to be suffering from delayed shock, which detached their minds from their surroundings and painted their eyes with a blurring glaze. Craig's melancholy face was turned toward the folded-over corpse of Jim Denby.

"Yeah, he was something else," Edge growled sardonically, not holstering the Remington as he retrieved his hat from the bunk behind Craig and crossed to put his back to the diminishing heat of the stove.

"I meant up until today, son," the older man augmented. "Of all the Bar-M hands who used to give us a hard time he was the best. If it hadn't been for him, that trigger-happy Reece would have . . . well, I don't know what would have happened." Craig shook his head, the sadness deepening in his bright blue eyes. "And you know, son, I don't reckon Jim Denby would have ridden off and left us with Reece. He'd have figured out somethin' else."

"His figuring days are over, old man," the half-breed said flatly. "He just didn't count on his number coming up."

Craig sighed and then shook his head, needing the physical gesture to rid his mind of futile reflections on the past and what might have been for the future. Just for a moment, as he became fully aware of the present, he was afraid. But then he looked at the tall, impassive faced half-breed and saw the gun in the brown-skinned hand and the unblinking, glittering slits of his eyes watching the closed door.

"Never did get through tellin' you about last night, did I, son?" he asked through the drifting blue tobacco smoke, the aroma of which had neutralized the taint of recent gunfire.

"Enough for me to know why Van Dorn and his partners happened to be in my way," Edge answered.

Craig ignored the implication of disinterest as he cupped the bowl of his pipe in both gnarled hands and stared down into the fading glow of the tobacco. "It was mighty tirin' work, shiftin' the shack in that storm. And after we'd done it we couldn't do nothin' else except hit the sack in the cave we'd been livin' in since the Bar-M boundary moved south.

"Sheep were corralled up real tight then. But come sunup they weren't there no more. And the neither was our shack, son. They'd taken off the tarps that were over all the stuff we'd moved and put a torch to it. That storm was finished by then. Which was how me and my buddies was able to track our flock and the men that was herdin' them."

There was no longer anger in Craig's tone and his expression was as lacking in emotion as his voice. Perhaps killings, old and new, had expunged his burning resentment. Or maybe it was just that the energy-sapping rigors of recent events had drained him of the capacity to experience deep feelings of any kind. Only rest and time would tell.

"Been thinkin' about that, son. Reason they didn't slaughter our animals right there and then. And left a trail a near blind man could follow. Can only be they figured to kill me and Lonny and Doug as well as the sheep. And wanted to have us and our animals a long ways into Bar-M range so they'd have some kind of excuse to give the law.

"Make any kinda sense, son?"

"Some," Edge allowed, listening hard to the wild sounds of the blizzard and trying to decide if they were diminishing.

"Might have done it, too. If Van Dorn and them other guys hadn't spotted you headin' toward them." He sighed. "Like Doug said, we been havin' a hell of a lot of good luck."

Silence intruded into the line shack then and without the distraction of Craig's voice the half-breed was able to concentrate on the mournful moaning of the wind, which was definitely losing force. And, by the same slow degree of change, the hurricane lamp became increasingly unnecessary as the daylight pressing through the windows got brighter.

The atmosphere in the shack grew colder as the fire in the stove died to embers that then disintegrated into ashes. The sheepmen turned up their collars and buttoned their coats.

There was no noticeable change in temperature when the door opened and the woman stepped inside ahead of the man. The snow was floating down now and the only flakes that came into the shack were on the boots of the couple. And on their hats and the blankets draped over their shoulders.

The woman was not surprised by the changes that had taken place since she was last in the shack; she seemed to be withdrawn into some kind of trance that had a pleasantly calming effect on her.

The man looked at Edge and the unaimed Remington with alarm and muttered: "Oh dear."

"Come on in," the half-breed invited. "You've already seen we don't go in much for good manners. No need to take off your hat."

The wryly spoken words, punctuated by the closing of the door, acted to bring the woman back into the real world.

The opening of the door had awakened the trio of sheepmen to the possible dangers that might still make this their last Christmas Eve.

"Daughter and I intend no harm to any of God's creatures," the priest said hurriedly. He clasped his pudgy hands together at his chest as his tiny green, flesh-squeezed eyes emanated sincerity. "Unless they mean to harm us," he added, even faster, after his gaze had fallen fleetingly on the pair of corpses.

"Father speaks the truth," the woman confirmed eagerly. "For that is his mission. To bring the truth to the people."

"I never did see no priest like him before," Bassett growled, but looked at the woman.

"Ain't that the truth," Smith countered, his voice a whisper of awe as he, too, gawked at her.

"I am an itinerant preacher of the word of God, gentlemen," the priest explained, unconcerned that the woman commanded most of the attention. "Who must by force of circumstances conform with the mores of my parish, which I consider to be the whole world."

Craig, always the most practical of the sheepmen, was able to shift his gaze away from the woman and perhaps wipe from his mind the memory of her naked torso. "People ain't supposed to kill people, are they?" he asked. "Ain't that God's word?"

"Then why did he allow man to invent instruments of death such as the gun?" the priest replied easily.

"Reckon he didn't, son," Craig argued, addressing a middle aged man who was probably less than ten years his junior. "That was the work of the devil." He glanced pointedly at the dyed blonde again. "Same as the sins of the flesh."

The priest pouted his lips even further than their natural set. "Nonsense, sir. If we are to believe God created all things in the universe, can we also think Him so stupid as to make such an adversary for himself? No, sir! God instilled both good and evil in His creatures. And those who would hear and understand His word use evil to sustain goodness."

"Amen," the woman agreed with great fervor.

"How's the evil you just committed with your daughter do any good, son?" Craig insisted earnestly.

The priest smiled and shook his head. The expression gave his fleshy features a quality of gentleness that, for the first time, gave him a priestly look that went beyond the mere fact of his clerical garb.

"I fear you have misconstrued our use of the terms father and daughter, sir," he explained. "I am, of course, a father to all who respect the cloth. Father Sean O'Keefe in full. And to me, all my converts are sons and daughters. My traveling companion, gentlemen, is Sara North. Known in the Virginia City establishment from which I rescued her as Angel North."

"She's a whore?" Bassett exclaimed.

The priest's gentle smile retained possession of his florid face. And, since he had spoken his name, the Irish brogue seemed to be thicker in his speech. "Was, sir. Until a few short weeks ago, Angel was indeed a member of the oldest profession."

"What is she now, son?" Craig asked as he and his partners looked again at the once-beautiful woman who was as serenely composed as the priest.

"My help in troubled times, sir."

"Comes from her keepin' all the tools of her old trade," Smith growled sourly.

"It is God's will," the priest countered, unperturbed by the sheepmen's attitude to his relationship with the former whore. "One of woman's functions is to provide comfort when man's road is long and tiring."

"Amen," the whore from Virginia City chanted. "My mission is to raise up the spirits of my father when they flag."

"And something else, I figure," Edge muttered, pushing the Remington into his holster. "Seeing as how you've got a crutch for him to lean on."

Chapter Six

THE superstitious belief of the heavily fleshed Doug Smith in the ability of fortune for good or ill to play a ruling part in his life had as its foundations the religious teachings of years in the distant past. And it was he alone who objected to the Irish priest and the ex-whore joining the ride away from the line shack after the blizzard had finally blown itself out.

Edge did not hear the sheepman voice his criticisms of the strange pair of evangelists. Nor see or hear the responses it drew from the couple and from Craig and Bassett. Because he was alone for several minutes in the stable out back of the shack, eating frugally from the sparse supplies in his saddlebags, before Owen Craig joined him.

"You as short of grub as me and my buddies are, son?" the wrinkle-faced old man asked earnestly.

"I got nothing to spare, feller."

Craig blew into his cupped hands and shook his head. "Ain't askin' for nothin'. Tryin' to tell you that unless you got plenty, you'd better head for Fallon same as we all are."

Edge lit a ready-rolled cigarette. "That God's will?" he asked wryly.

The sheepman grimaced. "Message from that screwball that reckons he's got a direct telegraph line to the Almighty, is all. But it ain't got nothin' to do with the man upstairs unless these blizzards are some kind of sign."

The half-breed peered out from the open doorway of the stable at the snow-covered mountain landscape under a brightening sky. "Covers sign is all, feller."

"What? Oh, yeah. But snow blocks trails, too. And O'Keefe reckons there ain't no way we're gonna get through Jason's Pass to reach Bredyville. Not until after the spring thaw, that is. He and his woman come through this mornin' and nearly didn't make it on account of last night's storm. Won't nobody make it after this new snow."

"No other way west, feller?"

"Jason's Pass is the only easy way when it's high summer, son."

"And Fallon's the only other place where I can get supplies around here?"

"Unless you count the Bar-M ranch." Craig grimaced again, the lines cutting deeper into skin hanging loosely on his facial bones.

"What's east along the trail that runs south of the range?"

"Fallon, is all. Heads east until the valley that bounds the property on that side. Then swings north, up through an old ghost town and northeast to Fallon. A long way round. Quickest route for us is to backtrack." He licked his lips. "That's all of us, if you decide to come along."

"No sweat, feller."

"Doug ain't too happy about O'Keefe and the woman. Used to have religion at one time. It don't bother you, son? The way them two talk and act?"

Snow had crunched under booted feet, the sound not loud enough to mask Craig's words from the ears of the newcomers. The priest and the one time prostitute looked in through the stable doorway.

"I trust you have no objections, sir?" O'Keefe asked.

The woman smiled beguilingly at Edge, in the inviting, professional manner of her former trade.

"Just as long as we get a couple of things straight at the outset, feller," the half-breed replied.

"Yes, sir?"

He nodded toward Angel North. "She should know I got nothing against whores. Never have and don't intend to start now."

If the woman was hurt by the barbed words, she showed no sign of it. She simply nodded, as calmly as did O'Keefe.

"The second, sir?"

"Applies to you. Don't ever point your hat at me."

They left a few minutes later, under an afternoon sky which was still gray with the weight of unfallen snow. But high to the west the cloud had a slick sheen where the sun was struggling to break through. They rode for a long time in silence. Then the priest and his woman began to talk. In low tones, but they did not seem deliberately to be guarding their conversation from the ears of Edge and the three sheepmen. Occasionally, a snatch of what they were saying could be heard and invariably it was in a religious vein. O'Keefe appeared to be continuing with his task of instructing his eager convert in the ways of her newly chosen life.

These overheard phrases served to strengthen Doug Smith's resentment, which, if the direction of his malevolent glances were a true indication of his feelings, was now aimed entirely at the unorthodox priest.

"Bullshit!" the fat sheepman blurted at length, unable to keep his rancor under control any longer.

He and Bassett were the back markers. O'Keefe and the woman rode ahead of them and Edge and Craig were in the lead.

The priest allowed the spitefully spoken interruption to curtail his flow and turned without anger to look levelly at Smith. "I do not deny a man the right to hold opinions different from my own, sir," he responded evenly. "I simply consider it my mission to try to change them."

Smith's several chins and heavy cheeks were quivering with indignation. "You did a fine job with Denby and Reece."

O'Keefe remained unruffled. "It would seem I did you and your friends a great favor."

The sheepman shook his head. "I ain't denyin' that, mister! But don't you try to pretend you did it in the Lord's name! You tricked 'em with the whore's body and then shot 'em down like dogs. You tryin' to make out that was God's will is what galls me!"

"How else can you explain it, sir? We were lost in the blizzard, without food or adequate clothing. And we stumbled on an ample supply of provisions and shelter. Daughter would gladly have paid for these comforts with her body. But her days of degredation are over now. I demand that she be given respect and treated with tenderness. The two men you speak of had no such intention. I'm sure your friends will agree?"

He looked expectantly at Bassett, Craig, then Edge.

Craig allowed: "Al Reece never did to my knowledge treat anybody or anythin' with respect."

He spat into the snow.

The priest nodded his satisfaction with the meager agreement of these words. "And I say again, it was God's will."

Smith spat, more forcefully than Craig.

"Somethin' else, Doug," Bassett put in thoughtfully.

"What?" the man riding at his side snapped.

"It all ties in with what Mr. Edge was sayin' early on this mornin.' It being Christmas Eve and all."

Abruptly he had the attention of all except Edge, who was almost totally immersed in his habitual exercise of checking the surrounding terrain for signs of danger. More so than usual now, as he got an inkling of what was on Bassett's mind and endeavored to bar the idea from his own.

"About Maria Lassiter expectin' a kid by a guy named Joseph. Us bein' sheepmen. Even Starr."

"Sir?" the priest asked, puzzled and becoming excited.

"What's that all got to do with it, Lonny?" Craig wanted to know. And in his voice and face there was a trace of nervousness.

"Look what's happened?" Bassett invited. "East wasn't the way we figured to head, was it? Yet we are. And a woman called Angel is along with us—told us there was no chance we could go the way we wanted."

"Please!" O'Keefe urged, as Smith stifled a scornful protest and became as nervously pensive as Craig and Bassett. "You are going too fast. I know none of this. Please tell me exactly what has happened. In detail."

"What do you think, son?" the man beside the half-breed asked as Bassett began to satisfy O'Keefe's eager curiosity. "You started us on this kick. Are we lettin' our imaginations run way with us or what?"

"I don't know, feller," Edge replied and tried again to use humor as a bar to the intrusion of unwanted thoughts. "But I figure we shouldn't believe anything Maria Lassiter says."

"How's that, son?"

"Won't be the first time a knocked-up spinster claims she's going to have a virgin birth."

Craig's reaction to the cynicism was a snort. Then he half-turned his head to listen to Bassett's amplification of the events of the morning and the answers he gave to O'Keefe's avidly interested questions.

When this was finished with, a new silence settled upon the group of riders moving slowly but inexorably through the deep snow. But there was no quality of acrimony insinuated in the atmosphere now. For the subject of their thoughts was too absorbing to admit side issues.

One woman and five men rode in close proximity to each other, yet were detached and alone on every level up from the merely physical. Five men because Edge, despite his attempts to contemplate only the practical reasons for reaching Fallon, was unable to remain unmoved by the possible consequences of the strange string of coincidences.

For several minutes he tried another line of defense against the persistent images of unreality, which sought entry to his mind: calling upon the experiences of the past to use self-anger at his inability to maintain his thought processes in the here and now of the real world. But this was as much a failure as cynicism had been.

And he was forced to acknowledge that the happenings of the day in which he had played a part could presage some world shattering event in the near future. And, as soon as he surrendered to this possibility, he experienced an easing of tension deep within himself.

The heavy frown, which had previously given his cold pinched face the rigid look of a wood carving, was abruptly transformed into an easy smile.

"Crazy," he said softly.

"Ain't it, though," Craig rasped.

But the half-breed had not been referring to the events that held the old man and the others in deep thought, rather to his own reaction to them. Or, rather, his conscious efforts not to react to them.

To himself he repeated the word with which Doug Smith had re-opened the subject: *Bullshit!* And grinned, the light in his narrowed, glinting eyes colder than the air pressing against his skin and the snow being crunched beneath the hooves of the gelding. Relieved to have beaten whatever power had tried to force unwanted ideas into his mind. For by allowing them entrance he was able to examine them calmly and dismiss them rationally.

Because his struggle to ignore them had given the ideas false importance and thus had he fallen into the dangerous trap of worrying about the unknown. And a vivid example of how dangerous this was had been his contemplation of death while he was a prisoner at the line shack.

By the very nature of the kind of man he had become, Edge had to be a realist in order to survive. For when death threatened, as it so often did, it was futile and defeatist to merely reflect upon it. And yet, that was what he had done, his normal objectivity clouded by abstract thought triggered by . . . bullshit.

Of the others riding through the fresh layer of snow spread upon the earlier fall the short and rotund priest was the first to emerge from the period of reflection.

"Hallelujah!" he proclaimed. "The hour of the second coming will soon be upon us! Let us give thanks to God and commune with him!"

Edge had dug the makings from a shirt pocket and was rolling a cigarette. "You want us to look the other way while you and the whore do that, feller?" he asked.

"The act which enables procreation is a wonderous thing, unbeliever!" O'Keefe countered, unperturbed by the half-breed's cynicism. "In worshipping the body of one's partner one is also worshipping the creator of such a wonderous thing. But there are many ways of praising the Almighty!"

"When the spirit's willing but the flesh is weak," Edge muttered, lighting the cigarette and peering north toward the timber-clad rise where he had first seen the trio of sheepmen.

"Let us pray, brothers!" O'Keefe invited. "We who have been chosen to witness the return of the Lord Jesus Christ to this sinful world."

"Yes, let us pray!" Angel North agreed with shrill eagerness. "Yes, yes!"

The priest with the gun inside his hat launched into a long and rambling prayer, his voice strong as he intoned the spontaneous words of praise and gratitude toward the empty sky and across the white barrenness of the country on all sides.

The sheepmen imitated the actions of O'Keefe and the woman by clasping their hands in front of their chests and screwing their eyes tight closed. Their horses continued to carry them north, the animals taking their lead from the gelding of the open-eyed, impassive-faced half-breed.

For perhaps thirty minutes the priest's stentorian voice rang out, never faltering as his theme switched from this Christmas to the first one, from this to the sins of the world at large and of the present company in particular, then back again.

Edge, concerned only with the stamina of his horse, his diminished supplies, the possibility of another blizzard, and the dangers of a run-in with another group of Bar-M hands, kept constant vigil on the convoluted whiteness that rolled away from him in every direction.

"Amen!" the priest concluded.

The woman echoed this and the sheepmen chorused it a moment later. Then a new verbal silence settled over the slow-moving group, far less heavy than that which had preceded O'Keefe's orison. It lasted for a long time, until the priest broke it as they started up the lower slope of the tree covered hill.

"There is no way that we can travel faster, I suppose?"

"Not unless you can arrange for the snow to thaw, feller" Edge answered.

O'Keefe nodded. "It was a foolish thing to ask. We have been shown too many signs. The Almighty will take account of the difficulties of our journey."

When the crest of the rise was reached the mood of the three sheepmen altered. They were close to the clearing where their animals were slaughtered and their eyes became dull as their mouths formed into expressions of remembered grief and anger. In the clearing, fresh snow had drawn a pure white blanket over the carcasses, concealing the ugly crusts of congealed blood and the sightlessly staring eyes of the wantonly killed sheep.

"What happened here?" O'Keefe asked, suddenly nervous as he looked from the bristled faces of Craig, Bassett, and Smith to the strangely humped layer of snow. Then: "Ah! This is where the killing of your animals took place. As Brother Bassett told me. But be comforted. Soon the Son of God will be amongst us again. And this time, surely, the evil that is in all men will be expunged for all time."

"Amen!" Angel North proclaimed.

But the memory of the brutal wrong done to them continued to claim the sheepmen's thoughts until the group moved out of the timber at the foot of the northern slope. Here, with no foliage to interrupt the fall, the new snow had completely covered the bodies of Van Dorn, Raven, and Starr, and to fill in the tracks left by the wanderings of the five Bar-M horses.

No mention was made of the shoot-out on the fringe of the timber and, as the group swung toward the valley marking the eastern extent of Lassiter range, the silence remained unbroken except by the crunch of snow beneath hooves. But no words were necessary. For, as the scene of former evil receded behind them, the sheepmen again became infected by religious hope for a future of heaven-sent good.

Behind them and to the right, the slick sheen of the sun trying vainly to punch a hole through the clouds sank lower down the western dome of the sky. And the brightness of its light grew inexorably dimmer. The approach of evening plunged the temperature of the mountain air to lower degrees of coldness. Frost began to sprinkle white crystals on the snow, on clothing, on the coats of horses, and even the bristles of men's faces. The air they breathed, unmoved by even the slightest stir of wind, seemed to form films of ice against the membranes of their lungs.

"We ain't gonna make Fallon tonight, son," Craig growled. "Not unless it gets warmer. We'll end up frozen stiff as old corpses."

"The Almighty will provide!" O'Keefe assured.

His voice, like that of Craig's, was given a tone of hoarseness by the bitterly cold flow of air through his throat. But whereas the sheepman spoke with the tough conviction of undeniable truth, the priest's words contained little force beyond hope.

"Just need for Him to hold off more snow for awhile," Edge said as the group reached the ridge overlooking the valley with the ghost town at its head.

The priest gazed down at the distant buildings huddled darkly against the snow and emanated fervent confidence again. "And He has provided, brothers! A place for weary travelers to rest and take shelter from the elements! How say you, daughter?"

"It's another sign, Father," the whore from Virginia City responded with a radiant smile. "Let's go fast so we can give our thanks!"

"What's wrong, son?" Craig asked anxiously when Edge made no move to heel his horse down the slope.

"Yeah, Edge!" Bassett urged. "Let's get over there before we all freeze to our saddles!"

"Just thinking it could be real warm in that town," the half breed answered.

"How's that, son?"

All of them were peering hard at Edge as he directed the stare from his slitted eyes toward the huddle of buildings.

"On account of there ain't no smoke without fire, feller."

Eyes shifted their puzzled gazes away from Edge to look at the town. For stretched seconds they failed to spot any movement. Then the woman caught her breath and the others stiffened and leaned forward. For a blur of darkness, which was not static, captured their attention. And they recognized it as a drifting wisp of black woodsmoke.

"Who can say that those who lit the fire mean us harm?" O'Keefe asked, looking anxiously at the half-breed, his tiny green eyes pleading for a reassuring answer.

"It's been that kind of day," Craig growled. "No reason to figure it's gonna get better."

"Place your trust in the Lord your God," the priest advised, his voice sounding less forceful than he had intended as Edge heeled his gelding forward to start down into the valley.

"Amen," Angel North added and even her one-word contribution lacked its previous fervor.

"What d'you reckon, son?" Owen Craig posed softly, his worried gaze fixed upon the smoke that rose slowly from out back of the saloon at the western end of the town's single street.

Edge looked from the frost-sprinkled face and form of the sheepman to rake his impassive gaze over the white wilderness of the snow-covered valley. "That it looks like hell's froze over, feller," he answered flatly. "And on the day that happens, ain't the impossible supposed to be possible?"

Whoever was tending the fire behind the saloon in the abandoned town had reached the shelter before the last blizzard ravaged the Wind River Mountains. Or at least before the last flakes of snow had fallen. For there was no sign to show the direction of approach.

The sheepmen, the priest, and the woman eased

their pace a little as the group closed with the town, by common and unspoken consent allowing the half-breed to move slightly ahead.

Edge approached the familiar buildings on the same line by which he had left that morning, the gelding carrying him out onto the street between the two houses diagonally across from the saloon. The big one-piece door of the building, which had provided him with shelter last night, was still open. The batwings were closed and unmoving. The doorway of the store across the alley in which Buel and Young had waited was also open to the elements.

The corpses of the two Lassiter hands might still have been on the street, buried by the new snowfall. And, as he dismounted, Edge recalled the undisturbed snow on the fringe of the timber and realized that the bodies of three other cowhands might have been moved. There had been no way to tell there, either.

He withdrew the Winchester from the boot before he started across the street, flexing his fingers to start the circulation flowing—the memory of what had happened at the line shack fleetingly but vividly crossing his mind. At the mouth of the alley he halted and listened, the smell of woodsmoke strong in his nostrils. The only sounds he heard came from behind him and he glanced over his shoulder. Craig, Bassett, and Smith were trailing him, stepping carefully into the depressions his own booted feet had made in the snow. The sheepmen were carrying their rifles.

The priest and his woman remained in their saddles. They seemed to be praying.

"The Almighty helps them that help themselves, ain't that so, son?" Craig whispered, hoarse and frightened.

"Fire's in the stove in the livery," the half-breed murmured.

"We can't go in shootin'," Smith said. "We don't

know who they are. We ain't on Lassiter range no more."

"The three of you want to go along the other side of the saloon?" Edge suggested.

Bassett licked his cold roughened lips and his tongue seemed to make a rasping sound. "What then?"

"Son?" Craig posed to the half-breed.

"It's polite to knock on a door when you know somebody's on the other side."

He started into the alley without giving the sheepmen a chance to respond, briefly conscious of their fear and confusion. Behind him, the three old men hesitated, unsure of how seriously to take Edge's words. Then Craig took the lead, across the front of the saloon and around the corner.

Most men have some kind of sixth sense, which warns them when watching eyes are upon them. And Edge had developed this sensitivity to a higher degree than most during the war and its aftermath. But experience had taught him that it was not something to entirely trust. Thus, as he moved along the alley through the snow and fast-falling dusk, his muscles were poised for instant response to the actions of others—be they good or evil. Even though he had failed to detect any intangible signs of being watched as he rode into town and then advanced on foot. For, as he had discovered already today, he was not always in control of the workings of his mind: at a conscious level and below.

The livery was directly behind the saloon, across a small yard once enclosed by a fence, which had rotted and crumpled. A large door, now firmly shut against the approaching night, faced the rear of the saloon. It had been open when Edge had led the gelding down the alley and out onto the street much earlier in the day.

He could recall clearly what lay on the other side of

the door. An aisle down the center from front to rear, with six stalls on either side. Against the back wall a pot-bellied stove with the stack still in place.

As he used a water butt to climb up onto the roof of the saloon, smoke continued to spiral up from the visible portion of the stack at the rear of the livery's roof. The heat of the fire in the stove below had melted some of the snow on the roof, but the freezing frost had arrested the process and laid a hard crust on the depleted layer that remained.

The snow on the saloon roof was twice as thick.

No lamp light or even fire glow showed at any of the cracks in the warped timber of the stable walls.

He had made fast time, moving as quietly as the frosted snow would allow. The three men walking on a similar surface on the other side of the saloon were slower and, necessarily, noisier. Each time their feet lowered into the snow the sound of the crunching frost and compacting flakes seemed loud enough to rouse the long-ago dead. When the white-sprinkled forms of the trio appeared below him, they looked like ghostly apparitions.

Edge remained silent as the men peered around, searching for him. Eventually, some inexplicable mechanism in their minds drew their puzzled gazes up toward him. He still failed to sense any other eyes surveying the yard and its surroundings.

Bassett opened his mouth to speak, but stayed silent when Edge pressed a stiff finger to his own lips. Despite the failing light, the fear was clear to see on the sheepmen's faces when the half-breed gestured for them to approach the livery door. Again he did not wait for their agreement or otherwise. Instead, he stretched out full length on the roof, behind the insubstantial cover of the line of undisturbed snow above the eaves.

"Hell, this is stupid!" Craig said, loud and harsh.

And above and behind the old man, Edge uttered a low grunt that could perhaps have indicated qualified agreement with the words.

More snow was crunched underfoot as Craig led the reluctant Bassett and Smith toward the livery.

"Hey, you inside! Got room for some real cold folks?"

Even had there been a friendly invitation to enter, the half breed would not have felt foolish; humiliated by his overreaction of caution. For it was his way and he had escaped death on countless occasions by guarding against danger in an apparently innocent situation. Often, as now, by putting the lives of others on the line.

No welcoming words were called from inside the livery. No words of any kind. No sound.

Edge grunted again, the small sound totally noncommittal now. He took a firmer grip on the Winchester, his index finger squeezing first pressure against the trigger. It was impossible to ignore the intense cold. All he could do was will his mind to remain detached from the possibility of frostbite and concentrate on the potentially much greater danger that threatened from below.

For he was certain now that the men on the other side of the livery door were not friendly. Men or man?

Soon he would find out, for Craig, Bassett, and Smith were at the door. Craig stood back a little with his Winchester aimed from the hip. The other two had their rifles in the crooks of their arms as they lifted the big iron latch.

Their minds would be working on the same line as the half-breed's.

The smoke had been rising from the stack at a constant rate since it had first been seen from the ridge of the valley side. So somebody had been feeding fuel to the flames.

Even if no watch had been maintained, the presence of newcomers was now a known fact. For, even if those inside had been sleeping, Craig's shouts would have awakened them.

Those shouts had committed the sheepmen to a course of overt action.

Bassett and Smith snapped up the latch and lunged backward, dragging the door open. The snow at its base was plowed into a higher pile and they got the door halfway open before further progress was blocked. The two men sat down hard.

Warm air tainted with the scent of tobacco smoke wafted out into the evening and was immediately cooled. The murky light of the dying day spread inside.

The only man it showed wore a deep cut expression of great pain. He had to make a great effort to force out the words: "Kill me, Craig, and you'll be doin' me a favor!"

"Lassiter!" Craig gasped.

He was an old man, made to look considerably older by recent pain and suffering. Tall and thin, like a starving giant. His face was long and gaunt with deep eye sockets and sunken cheeks. His hair was white and sparse, except where it grew as a well-trimmed goatee from the point of his long jaw. He was at the rear of the stable, sprawled limply, almost lifelessly, on a bed of many blankets in front of the stove.

"And you'll be dead right after," another man threatened.

"All three of you," another added.

"Them that are with you."

"If that's the way you want it."

The warnings, called flatly from many points inside the stable, froze Bassett and Smith in the process of struggling to get double handed grips on their rifles.

"Kill them now!" Cole Lassiter snarled. "Kill those murderin', sheep-screwin' bastards!"

"No, sir. That ain't our way."

This from the man who had first threatened to avenge the old man's death. He spoke from one of the stalls on the left. Just his head and shoulders showed above the timber partition. He was aiming a a rifle from his left shoulder. Other men showed themselves in a similar fashion in other stalls. A dozen in all.

"Damn you, I'm givin' you an order!" Lassiter roared.

Eleven of the riflemen stood like mute statues. The twelfth moved only his lips. "We ain't killers. Unless we gotta defend ourselves. Could've blasted you men long before you got this close."

"C.B.'s right," Craig rasped to his partners, and allowed the muzzle of his Winchester to dip toward the snow. "And he was always fair with us."

Cole Lassiter moved only his head, swinging it frantically to left and right to direct the enraged stare of his blazing eyes toward the unresponsive backs of his men. Watching him and seeing the limpness of the man's limbs and body, Edge got the impression that, even had he wanted to, Lassiter could not have moved any other muscles except those controlling his neck.

"You double-crossin' bastards!" the helpless man by the stove roared.

He continued to be ignored.

"We seen six of you ridin' into the valley, Craig," the man called C.B. said evenly. "If the other three are givin' you cover—"

Footfalls crunched snow in the alley between the saloon and the store, the sound curtailing the man's new warning. Some of the Bar-M hands craned forward, Winchesters swinging toward the new targets.

"It's a woman!" somebody yelled.

"Maria?" Lassiter gasped.

"No, sir," C.B. replied, after a cursory survey of O'Keefe and Angel North.

"We are not welcome here?" the priest asked nervously. "We heard voices but no gunfire and—"

"One more, Craig," C.B. cut in on explanation.

"Don't trust them!" Lassiter snarled. "They killed your buddies. Van Dorn and Raven and Starr. Maybe Wes Young and Ben Buel for all we know! You can't—"

"We can, sir," C.B. interrupted calmly. "It's you who can't . . . do anythin'. Except talk and maybe that's bad for you." His voice became harsher. "Well, Craig? You're one short. And you can see there's twelve of us."

"Edge!" Craig yelled and his partners took their cue from him in not turning to look up at the saloon roof. "If they wanted us dead, son, we'd already be that way."

The half-breed scowled his reluctant acceptance that he had no alternative but to surrender once more to Bar-M cowhands. And turned his rifle to toss it, two-handed, down into the snow. A dozen Winchesters and as many tense faces swung toward the spot where it thudded. Daylight was almost exhausted now and the men in the stable were unable to judge precisely the position from which the rifle had been thrown.

Snow crunched as Edge got to his feet, drawing the cautious eyes and menacing rifle muzzles toward him. They tracked him as he stepped off the roof and dropped sure footed to the soft ground.

"Aim the guns someplace else and never point them at me again," he said evenly. "Or squeeze the triggers now. Try to give folks the warning."

"You ain't in no position to be givin' orders, mister!" a man in the same stall as C.B. barked.

"Shut up, Hardin'!" C.B. snapped, and shouldered his rifle. Then, to Edge: "All right, mister. You're a real hard sonofabitch. We ain't no soft pricks, neither. But we reckon there's been enough killin' for one day."

His eyes shifted in their sockets to direct his words at everyone outside. "So you folks wanna come in? Warm yourselves and maybe eat somethin' hot. We don't want no trouble with you, unless you start it."

He and two other Bar-M hands seemed relieved that the sentiment had been spoken. The rest remained rigid with tension. Cole Lassiter's eyes stared at C.B. from out of a bottomless pit of hatred.

"You won't get no trouble from me and Lonny and Doug," Craig responded and started into the livery, still carrying his rifle. His two partners followed him.

"God is good and shares his goodness among many of his creatures," the priest blurted and took the woman's arm to guide her across the yard.

"Amen," she agreed gratefully and her perfect teeth added radiance to her smile again.

"Come on in, mister," C.B. invited. "I'll have a couple of the guys take care of your horses. Put them in the church with ours. This stable's the only place in town with a stove that still works."

"Obliged," Edge said, and stooped to pick up his rifle, holding it one-handed around the frame.

Some of the Winchesters, which had wandered off-target as the men holding them peered through the darkness at Angel North, were abruptly brought back to the aim.

"Relax, you guys!" C.B. urged. "Hardin', Turner, go fix up their horses."

The two men designated for the chore resented it. But C.B. was firmly in command and they trudged out into the snow. Edge held back for them to come out, then stepped over the threshold and pulled the door closed.

"Daughter!" the priest rasped.

"Yes, Father?"

"Don't you see? It's a stable! We have come from the west to the east to find ourselves in a stable!"

Somebody struck a match to light a lamp. Then another. They were hung on hooks designed to support harness. Looks of carnal interest, which had been directed through the murk at the woman were abruptly transformed into quizzical frowns as attention was diverted to the priest.

"Yes, Father," the woman agreed, a little breathlessly. She gazed about her with bright, excited eyes. "It will be here, I feel it."

"What the hell are they yakkin' about?" a man croaked.

"What kinda people you ridin' with, Craig?" C.B. asked.

"Well, you see, it's Christmas . . . !" the eldest sheepman started.

"And," Edge drawled as he advanced on the rear of the stable, "we got us some nuts."

Chapter Seven

THERE was a pile of recently cut and split logs behind the stove. As the half-breed moved closer to the helpless Lassiter, the sardonic words he spoke captured suspicious attention. But, once he had leaned his rifle against the wall and started to stoke the fire in the stove, the eyes of all the Bar-M men returned hurriedly to locate O'Keefe and Angel North.

For what seemed a long time, perhaps little more than a minute, the priest held his entire new audience as he launched into an amplification of his reference to the Nativity.

During this time, the half-breed continued to add logs to the stove and draw flames from the embers. And the sheepmen came deeper into the livery to share in the benefit of the heat. But then interest began to wane, as most of the hard-bitten cowhands scowled their scorn for what O'Keefe was saying and moved out of the stalls to form a group in front of the stove.

Cole Lassiter was among those who continued to be enthralled by the priest's words, cursing and glowering at any of his men who wandered across his restricted line of vision to O'Keefe. Four cowhands maintained an equally high level of interest. One of them crossed himself when O'Keefe unfastened his topcoat to reveal the clerical garb beneath.

Edge listened to the earnestly spoken words—without appearing to show any interest—for just long enough to ensure that the priest had presence of mind not to refer to the killings.

The voice of C.B. Wilder, foreman of the Bar-M, cut in on the half-breed's thoughts. "Your name's Edge?"

He spoke the name as if he were not entirely certain he had got it correct.

"Sure."

The half-breed looked at the man who had dropped to his haunches beside him. He was in his mid-forties with a darkly tanned, rough-hewn face cut with many lines that all curved downward. He was a sad-looking man. Short but broadly built with a suggestion of great physical strength. Little natural intelligence was visible in his dark eyes.

"Don't guess you know anythin' about doctorin'?" the melancholy man asked morosely.

"No, feller. But I figure your boss is in a bad way."

"We know that!" another man growled.

Except for the priest, the woman, and their five-man attentive audience, everyone else in the stable was gathered around the stove. Edge and the sheepmen were closest to the source of heat. Apart from Wilder squatting beside the half-breed, all the others were standing.

Wilder glowered at the speaker and lowered his voice. "He's too old to be out in this kinda weather. From what that crazy priest's been sayin', I guess you know why he come. Lookin' for Maria, his daughter."

"It ain't just a chill he's got, feller," Edge said evenly.

Wilder nodded. "Heart seizure or somethin'."

"Can't be nothin' wrong with his heart," Doug Smith rasped venomously. "He ain't never had one."

"That ain't so, Doug!" Craig countered, with a tone of sincerity that indicated he was not moved to speak entirely because of the dangerous looks directed at his partner by some of the Bar-M hands. "We got along with him and his men before he heard about Maria being pregnant."

"Easy," Wilder said placatingly, sharing a sad-eyed look between his own men and the newcomers. Then he gazed fixedly at Craig. "What's done is done. There's been killins today. In this town and out at the timber where your animals were slaughtered, I guess you're responsible for some of it, maybe all of it. I ain't askin'. Maybe the law will want to know about it but that'll be between you and the territorial peace officers. I seen your sheep dead out there and probably you had good cause to kill Van Dorn and Raven and Starr."

"Jimmy Raven was a good friend to me," a man snarled softly into the silence as Wilder paused and O'Keefe completed his oration.

"Shut up," the Bar-M foreman chided flatly. "It's done, like I said. As for Buel and Young—well, maybe the girl's guy killed them. I dunno. But that don't matter neither. Not right now it don't."

"You will excuse daughter and I," O'Keefe requested of Cole Lassiter and the other four men who had been paying such close attention to him. "But we must give thanks to the Almighty for his guidance and protection, which brought us to this place. And we must do this in private."

"Amen," came the familiar response, as the brightly smiling, eager-eyed former whore allowed herself to be ushered into a stall.

"Then what the hell is important, C.B.?" a man asked hoarsely.

"Bring my daughter to me!" Cole Lassiter demanded. His voice was also hoarse. But he did not have to make any effort to keep his tone low. Fear distorted his pained face as he turned to look at his men and the newcomers. "Dear God, my voice is goin' as well," he whispered.

He wrenched his head around to its fullest extent, his pleading eyes raking across every face.

"Please?" The single word was almost inaudible. "Maria?"

The stable door was wrenched open and a stream of bitingly cold night air streamed in, instantly disseminating the stove heat, which had begun to warm the atmosphere and raise damp steam from sodden clothing. Harding and Turner entered quickly and closed out the night.

"Sonofabitch!" the hard-eyed, thin-lipped Harding exclaimed as he did a double take into the stall occupied by O'Keefe and Angel North. "They're screwin'!"

The fleshy-faced, broad-shouldered and narrow-waisted Turner whirled around to stare incredulously into the stall. Slowly, both men's expressions of disbelief were replaced by leering grins.

Edge and the three sheepmen sensed the swell of sexual excitement in the men around the stove.

"It's their way of thankin' the Almighty, C.B.," Craig said quickly.

"But he don't like anyone else doin' it," Bassett added. "To her."

There were no vocal sounds from the stall. Just a frenetic rustling of fabric as the coupling priest and his woman thrust and pulled toward a climax.

Then Angel North gasped, "Praise to the Lord!"

"Christ will be born again!" O'Keefe exclaimed.

Both of them stood up then, fully clothed, their faces above the stall side glowing with a brand of excitement that owed little to the act they had just completed.

"Well, I'll be!" Turner growled, awe replacing the leer on his face. "If that don't beat all the ways I heard of gettin' a woman to come across."

"Brothers!" O'Keefe proclaimed, almost comically diminutive beside the statuesque tallness of the woman.

"Daughter and I are happy to be in the family of God. And are not a man and a woman at their happiest in the act of procreation?"

"They ain't really pa and daughter," Bassett hastened to explain.

Harding was shaking his head slowly from side to side as he continued to stare at the strangely paired couple. "It's a priest!" he muttered. "Now I seen everythin'!"

"No, sir!" O'Keefe corrected as he ambled out of the stall, his pants fly securely fastened. "That is the Almighty's prerogative alone. But the signs predict that we shall be privileged to witness something for which the world has waited centuries."

"Maria!" Cole Lassiter forced out through teeth clenched against pain. "Please. Before I die."

The priest strained to hear the words down the length of the livery. Then, with his pouting lips quivering and his tiny eyes gleaming with a greater intensity of religious fervor, he lunged forward.

The Bar-M men made to swing their rifles at him. But arrested their moves when they saw O'Keefe drop to his knees beside Lassiter and gaze into his face.

"Maria? Your daughter? She is close by, sir? She can be brought here to this stable?"

Lassiter's mind was still receptive and capable of thought beneath the sea of pain that was washing through it. Whether or not he could recall recent events and understood O'Keefe's motives, it was impossible to guess. But he had sufficient awareness to recognize a man who wanted the same thing he did. And his lips moved in a vain attempt to plead for help. Spittle ran from one corner of the mouth suddenly dragged downward by the involuntary force of a muscle. More bubbled saliva gurgled in his throat. No words emerged. The dark eyes remained locked on the priest's face, transmitting a pitiful plea for help.

As Angel North dropped to her knees and clasped her hands together in front of her full breasts, O'Keefe laid a comforting hand on the dying man's shoulder. Then raised his head to look at the face of every other man in the stable.

"Maria must be brought here!" he announced firmly.

"That's what I had in mind, priest," Wilder said morosely.

"Then go bring her, sir!"

"From where?" He stood up.

O'Keefe pointed a shaking finger at Edge, who was smoking a freshly rolled cigarette. "He says she is in the town of Fallon!"

Although it was still impossible to tell what retentive powers were commanded by Lassiter's agonized mind, it was evident he understood the words being spoken. For now his pathetically pleading eyes swung to look at Edge and then C.B. Wilder.

The mournful foreman turned his head to look down at Edge. "I ain't askin' how you know, mister, but I gotta be sure you're sure."

"Where they said they were heading, feller," the half-breed replied.

Wilder nodded, the gesture seeming to lock his resolution more firmly. "Then that's where I'm headin'." He shifted his sad eyes to the upturned face of the dying man. And saw gratitude, more explicit than if it had been spoken, shining through the ugly sheen of pain on Cole Lassiter's skeletonized face. "We owe that to the poor bastard," the Bar-M foreman murmured.

"In this damn awful weather, C.B.?" the hard-eyed Harding snarled.

Wilder glanced around and saw that the majority of the men were of the same opinion as Harding. But that four of them—those who had been as enthralled by O'Keefe's story as Lassiter—nodded their approval of the foreman's plan.

"I ain't sayin' I go for the crazy tale this priest's been tellin'," Wilder announced. "Just aim to do a favor for a boss that was always a good and reasonable one until lately. And I ain't givin' no orders. Go to Fallon on my own if I have to. Glad to have company if anyone's a mind. But somebody'll have to stay here and see Mr. Lassiter's all right. Rest should go back and take care of the ranch."

"Hell, C.B.," Turner countered. "How d'we know it won't be a wild goose chase? We only got the stranger's word about Fallon."

The half-breed turned his head to look coldly at the broad-shouldered, narrow-waisted cowhand. "Been known to lie when there's good reason, feller," he said, crushing out his cigarette on the floor. "Only reason I might do it now is to get some of that hot food I heard about."

"That sure would go down a treat, son," Craig said enthusiastically.

"To you, maybe," Edge responded. "I always pay my way."

"Up to you, mister," Wilder allowed. "But I figure to have John Groves fix me up some T-bones and grits before I leave. And all you folks are welcome to join me."

"Sure, C.B."

The man who spoke and stepped into one of the stalls where the gear of the Bar-M hands was piled was as short as O'Keefe but had an even greater girth. He was one of those who had been deeply moved by the priest's belief in the second coming and his round, pockmarked face still wore a pensively rapturous expression. He set about his cooking chore with his mind obviously on other things.

"We are indeed fortunate to have the Almighty's blessings showered upon us, daughter," O'Keefe enthused as he rose to his feet after giving Lassiter's shoulder a reassuring pat.

"That we most certainly are, Father," Angel North agreed as she moved to stand beside him and tower above him.

Both of them watched with great eagerness as the Bar-M cook prepared the food.

"Seems you got more blessins than most men, priest," Harding growled, his carnal desires roused again as he drank in the sight of the woman's body in profile against the light of one of the lamps.

Turner and some of the other men, perhaps long starved of the company of the opposite sex, were infected by Harding's mood and altered their positions to improve their view of the thrusting and flaring curves of Angel North's torso, half exposed by the low cut of the dress's neckline.

"Easy, you men!" Wilder growled, his words seeming to crackle through the almost palpable tension that had impregnated the stove-heated atmosphere of the livery.

"Hell, C.B.," Harding said softly, unable to wrench his eyes away from the twin swells of the woman's breasts. "What d'you expect us to feel like after him and her did it right here in front of us."

"They got a religious reason!" the foreman snapped as the woman remained calm and O'Keefe began to dart nervous glances around. "Sounds real blasphemous to me, but if that's their way then—"

"Shit, C.B.," Turner cut in, his lascivious grin broadening. "It ain't nothin' of the sort. We're with the priest. The way to heaven is up between a woman's legs."

He laughed and some of the others joined him. It made an ugly sound.

All the men had rested their rifles but wore gunbelts with Frontier Colts in the holsters. Three of the Bar-M hands drew in unison, leveling their guns at the backs of the amused group. The cook pulled and aimed his revolver as all attention was diverted from the woman by the metallic clicks of hammers being cocked.

"Tarnished she may be, but she's the Angel we need." This from the eldest of the cowhands, who wore thin-rimmed eyeglasses perched precariously on the crooked bridge of his nose.

"There's been too many signs to ignore." From a fresh-faced youngster with bright red hair.

The other man who had been convinced by O'Keefe wore long sideburns, which expanded into a bushy black beard at his jaw. He merely gave a curt nod of agreement with the others.

The hands who had been lusting for the woman were suddenly afraid as they looked from the three leveled guns to the Colt in Groves's fist. Then they raised their eyes to glance at the determination on the faces of O'Keefe's quartet of converts.

The priest was still nervous. Angel North remained serene.

Cole Lassiter managed to vent a low sigh and this seemed to signal relief to flow across the faces of the sheepmen and C.B. Wilder.

Edge appeared impervious to everything except the almost painfully appetizing aroma of frying steak, which rose from the skillet on the stove.

"Hell!" Harding croaked, and cleared his throat with a laugh. "We was only kiddin'."

"Just like Cole Lassiter's daughter is due to do," Craig interjected, and his laughter took more effort than Harding's had.

His joke drew flint-eyed stares from the gun toting men.

"Put the irons away, you men," Wilder instructed. "Let's eat. Okay, Harding? Turner? Trotter?"

His gaze drifted around the faces of the men who no longer expressed any trace of lust.

"Sure," one of them spoke for the others. And stared with something close to admiration from the short, fat, unattractive O'Keefe to the tall, fine-figured and once beautiful Angel North. "She's his and I swear I don't know why or how. But I take my hat off to him."

"Be glad he didn't take his off to you, feller," Edge muttered.

"What?" somebody asked.

O'Keefe glowered at Edge, then leaned closer to the stove and drew in a deep, noisy breath. "My, that smells good," he said quickly.

The cook shoved his Colt back into the holster and began turning the steaks in the skillet. "It ain't much, Father," he apologized.

"I'm so hungry I could eat just about anything, sir," O'Keefe assured. "How say you, daughter?"

"Whatever the Lord provides, Father," she answered.

Edge showed a sardonic grin to the earnest cook. "No sweat, feller," he drawled. "You already saw the priest and his woman have got catholic tastes."

Chapter Eight

AS C.B. Wilder led the group of riders out of the ghost town and onto the trail that cut southeast from the head of the valley, the cloud cover began to break up. The crescent of a young moon showed its blurred shape against the northern sky and, as it gradually became more clearly defined, the diamond-bright pinpricks of stars appeared.

The air flowing across the faces of the men got noticeably warmer.

"It's another sign!" the priest exclaimed, his tone brought close to a squeal by his delight. "Praise be to God for making our journey easier!"

He and Angel North were the back markers. Ahead of them rode John Groves and the redheaded youngster whose name was Willie French. In front of this pair were Wilder and Edge, the half-breed riding to the left and slightly behind the Bar-M foreman.

"It surely is a strange night," Groves mused, eyeing his surroundings of the snow-covered slopes and ridges with something close to awe. "First we get a hard frost under heavy cloud. Now it's gettin' clear as a bell and yet there ain't no frost no more."

"We can do little but wonder at the workings of the Almighty!" O'Keefe announced.

"Amen," the woman added.

Groves and French were a little late and a little self-conscious in voicing the sentiment.

"Groves is right," Wilder said softly after gazing up at the fast clearing sky. "I ain't never seen the weather do this before in these mountains."

"Don't let them get to you, feller," Edge advised without interrupting his less than wide-eyed surveillence of the now brightly moonlit whiteness of the terrain. "At least let there be two wise men when we reach Fallon."

In his own mind he was not entirely certain of the wisdom of his decision to join those heading for Fallon at this hour of the night. For, despite the slight improvement in the weather, it was cold and uncomfortable in the saddle. Especially with the memory of the livery stable still fresh.

Replete with food and warmer than he had been since leaving the line shack, the half-breed had been tempted to remain in the ghost town until morning, in company with the paralyzed and dying Cole Lassiter, the three sheepmen, and the other two Bar-M hands who felt there was going to be something different about this Christmas.

And there was no logical reason why he had not decided to do just this after the rest of the cowhands had ridden off into the night toward the greater comfort of the ranch house in the west. For it would have been easy for him to detach himself from the others—gone to sleep, even—in order not to be drawn into the incessant, fervid talk of what this coming Christmas day might bring.

He had simply made a snap—uncharacteristically impulsive?—decision to ride for Fallon. He could not recall that at the time he had thought of C.B. Wilder as his last human link with cynical reality. Or that Fallon beckoned because it was not a ghost town temporarily inhabited by a bunch of religious nuts but instead promised to be a community peopled with hard-bitten realists who would remain unaffected by the maniac beliefs of O'Keefe, Angel North, and their converts.

But, even now, as the group attained the ridge on the east side of the valley and Wilder pointed the way northeast along a trail he knew to be under the snow, Edge could fasten upon only a lame excuse for joining the night ride.

His tobacco poke was almost empty.

"He was never a bad guy before," the Bar-M foreman intruded on to the half-breed's rambling, disturbing thoughts.

Edge welcomed the opening after a long period of verbal silence. "Lassiter?"

"Yeah. Hard as Wind River ice this time of year. But a whole lot easier to see through. Had to be tough in his younger years to build up his spread. But after that it was always just an act."

"Happens sometimes when men get old," Edge offered. And, just for a moment, contemplated his own senility. But he dismissed the thoughts even before C.B. spoke, with the long-held conviction that he would never live into old age.

"Everythin' he did since Emmy Lassiter died was for Maria. Proudest day of his life was when he sent her off to some fancy school back East. Was always plannin' how she'd get a fine education, marry well, and her and her husband would come to the Bar-M and run it after he pegged out. That's a bad thing to do, ain't it, Edge?"

"What?"

"Try to live other folks lives for them?"

"Yeah," the half-breed agreed, then added cryptically, "It ain't been good for me, living some other feller's life."

Wilder gave him a long, quizzical look. But, from the set of the hawklike, heavy-bristled profile of the man, knew the soft-spoken comment was not to be expanded. "Cole Lassiter bein' that way about her, it figured there'd be a blow-up when he heard what happened to Maria. That she'd quit school and finished up in Denver, pregnant by some two-bit railroad worker.

"It seemed like he went off his head." Wilder snapped his fingers. "Changed, just like that. Gave hell to all of us that worked for him. Lot worse for Craig and his two partners. I tried to talk sense into him, on account of he'd always listened to me. But not any more. Decided he couldn't trust me. Anythin' lousy he wanted done, he'd talk straight to the men. The kind that'd do anythin' for a bonus. Like Harding. And Van Dorn. And Ben Buel.

"I knew Bar-M hands had been stirrin' up trouble for the sheepmen. But I didn't find out about the slaughter of the animals until it was done." Wilder paused, a grimace of revulsion cutting deep lines into his mournful face. "That was bad enough. But what he told Buel and Wes Young to do was a whole lot worse."

The man paused again, as if he had to take time to summon up the courage to speak the words.

"Kill Joe Redeker," Edge supplied.

Wilder gasped. "How . . . ?" Then he nodded. "You knowin' that means you were in that ghost town once before."

"This morning, feller. And all last night. The girl was ready to blow her brains out. Redeker involved me so I had to blast Buel. He took care of Young himself."

There was another long interlude in the conversation, during which it was obvious that the quartet riding behind were listening to the talk.

The foreman sighed. "Don't guess a guy like you would, but you needn't lose no sleep about killin' Ben

Buel. Pity Wesley Young had to die. He wasn't a bad guy."

"It is worthy to use evil in the cause of good," O'Keefe intoned.

"Obliged," Edge answered sardonically.

Wilder ignored the exchange as he veered his mount to the right, following the hidden trail down into a curving canyon. "Cole Lassiter was like a cat on hot bricks all today. Worryin' about why Buel and Young hadn't brought Maria to him, I found out later. When he couldn't take it no longer, he had all of us that weren't out line ridin' and fence fixin' mount up and leave the ranch. He didn't give a damn about the three men we found dead out on the range. Just told us about the killin' of the sheep. But when we found Buel and Young it hit him real hard. Hard enough to knock him off his horse and get sick the way you saw him.

"It was startin' in to snow again then. Like you saw at first, he was still givin' orders. Wanted us to ride every which way lookin' for Maria and the guy with her. But even if he was strong as before, weren't no man he'd have got to go out in that blizzard. So I decided we should hole up in the livery stable for the rest of the day and night.

"He hated us all for that. Me the most, but I knew he was sick. And now I'm sure he ain't gonna get well again, I reckon I owe him this much I'm doin' for him."

"Brother!" the priest said loudly, his voice echoing off the rock walls of the canyon, "even if the man were dead, the woman must be brought to the stable!"

"Amen," came the inevitable response from Angel North.

"Sure hope the onery old bastard lives," Wilder murmured.

The legs of the six horses continued to sink as deeply as ever into the snow. But the flakes were packed less firmly than before so that the going was easier. The sound of crunching snow was counterpointed by the steady drip of water from the canyon rims.

"I ain't never known a thaw this early in winter," Wilder rasped.

"Do not question it, sir," O'Keefe urged.

Beyond the canyon the trail dipped down a slope and then swung almost due east along a shallow valley. At the far end of it, perhaps a mile distant, a light shone brightly on a much higher level than the valley bottom.

"It was the wrong stable, Father!" Angel North gasped. "The star in the east!"

The priest crossed himself, which was the first genuinely religious gesture he had made.

Wilder turned his head to direct a scowl back over his shoulder. "That's the lamp that lights the sign of the Fallon Hotel, lady," he growled.

"And first time around there wasn't any room at the inn," Edge reminded flatly.

A kind of reverent silence was clamped over the group as the riders progressed slowly toward the light. And despite his earlier, almost involuntary decision to dismiss the seemingly divine overtones to so many recent incidents, the half-breed discovered he was again strangely disturbed by being a component part of this Christmas Eve in Wyoming.

A sidelong glance at C.B. Wilder showed that the mournful face was set in a frown of unease.

The valley along which they were riding deadended at another, which ran from north to south, and the town of Fallon was perched high on the eastern slope of the latter. It was a recently built town of brick and timber buildings flanking several broad streets laid out in a grid pattern. The light at the midtown section continued to gleam warmly. Until it abruptly took on a quality of cold, false hope: when the riders from the ghost town saw the river that barred their access to Fallon.

"Sonofabitch!" Wilder exploded. "Will you look at that John? And you, Willie! The Wind River ain't never like that until spring thaw!"

He had to shout to be heard above the roar of the torrential, white-lashed water that raced in a fury of frenetic movement in front of and below them.

By some strange trick of the Rocky Mountain terrain, they had been unable to hear the thunderous noise of the flooding river until they reached the end of the east-west valley. And looked down into the deeper depression that ran from north to south.

"It has to be twice as high as normal, C.B.," the fat cook of the Bar-M yelled.

"And runnin' ten times as fast!" the youthful French added.

Wilder shook his head in disbelief. "At Christmastime, yet! There ain't no way we're gonna cross it like that."

"Nonsense!" O'Keefe bellowed. "The Almighty will provide."

He heeled his horse forward and Angel North hurried to ride at his side, the two of them driving their mounts dangerously fast down the steep slope toward a darkened building less than twenty feet from the new level of the river.

"How's it usually crossed?" Edge asked after a narrow-eyed survey of the swollen river, the town on the opposite slope and the towering, jagged, snow-cloaked ridge above the town.

"You can ford it in summer!" Wilder shouted in reply. "By Doniphan's Ferry when it's too deep for that!"

"That's the Doniphan house!" Willie French yelled, pointing down at the unlit building in front of which

O'Keefe and Angel North were dismounting. "Old Ralph won't cross tonight!"

"Have faith, Willie!" John Groves urged, and heeled his horse down the slope.

The youngster eyed the rushing water anxiously, then sighed and took off in the wake of the fat man.

"Thought that crazy priest reckoned the thaw was supposed to help us?" Wilder growled. "What's he gonna do now? Fix it for the water to open up so we can just ride over?"

"That was by the feller they found in the bull-rushes," Edge answered, not loud enough for his reply to be heard above the thunder of the river as he urged his gelding down the slope. "O'Keefe figures we're getting close to the walking on the water time."

Wilder yelled at his horse to catch up with the half-breed and they reached the front of Ralph Doniphan's house as two splashes of light fell from windows. And they joined the still-mounted Groves and French in watching as the priest continued to thud his fists against the door. Angel North stood serenely at his side.

The noise of the river was much louder down close to its bank. Spray from the furious torrent was flung high and drenched across the newcomers. A long, flat-bottomed boat was leaning against the timber-side of the house, turned upside down to keep earlier snow and the later water out of it.

A new wedge of light sprang out into the night as the door was wrenched open from inside.

"What in hell's tarnation is all the damn noise about?" a man roared as his tall, broad frame became a dark silhouette against the lamplight behind him.

A shriller but less powerful voice—that of a woman—was indistinct from within the house.

"Sir, I and my companions must cross this river!" O'Keefe shouted. "Kindly make ready your boat!"

Ralph Doniphan was attired for bed in an all-engulfing white nightgown. Just for a moment it seemed not to hang loosely over his towering frame. Instead appeared to bulge with every line of his body as rage caused him to pull himself rigidly erect.

"Do what?" he thundered. And again there was a moment of hallucination when the volume and power of his voice seemed to drive the rushing river into frightened silence.

"Ralph!" The woman's voice was a mere scratch on the actual silence pervading the house.

"Make ready your boat, sir!" O'Keefe replied, necessarily loud but lacking any rancor in face of Doniphan's rage. He raised a hand as if to doff his low-crowned hat. "Or allow I and my companions to take it!"

He jerked the revolver free of its clamps and aimed it at the chest of the big man. Calm as the woman now, he put the hat back on his head.

"Have pity!" Angel North pleaded. "You will feel nothin'! But it will cause Father great hurt to have to kill you, sir!"

"Brothers, take the boat to the water!" O'Keefe called.

"It's my livin'!" Doniphan roared, suddenly bewildered and afraid. "That boat's my livin'!"

"We're with you, Father!" John Groves asserted, and jabbed young French in the ribs before he swung to the ground.

Wilder and Edge remained astride their horses as French dismounted and ran to catch up with the fat cook. The foreman appeared to be totally immobilized by the scene in front of him. Edge deliberately unfastened the buttons of his coat.

"Emily!" Doniphan roared, abruptly emerging from the same kind of incredulous analgesia that continued to grip Wilder.

O'Keefe had turned away from the door to check that Groves and French were doing what he had asked.

Doniphan swung a hand behind him, then thrust it forward. It was fisted around the butt of a long-barrelled revolver.

"You—" he started.

"Father!" Angel North shrieked.

The ferryman had a momentary advantage, but the watching half-breed was certain he would lose it. For it was a situation with which Edge was very familiar. Two men with guns. One of them with no regard for human life. The other who cherished his own existence and could not, perhaps only for the briefest of moments, end that of another without considering the terrible consequences.

The priest had merely to snap his head around. The Frontier Colt was still on target. He squeezed the trigger.

The big Ralph Doniphan fell back inside the house and a woman screamed.

"Oh, my God!" C.B. Wilder cried, and slammed his heels against the flanks of his mount to send it snorting toward the house.

The scream of the woman changed tone into a wail—like that of an animal in excruciating pain.

"It had to be done!" Angel North shouted to Groves and French who had skidded to a sudden halt at the sound of the shot.

The two Bar-M hands stared at each other, their bewildered minds struggling to reconcile violent death with their supposedly divine mission.

The fat cook with the pockmarked face died first. The young redhead a moment later. Their clothing and flesh shreaded and sprayed more forcefully across the snow than the spume from the raging river. Both of them blasted from close range by charges from a double barreled shotgun.

It was fired from the window by which they had halted, the first shot shattering the pane so that flying shards of glass added to the mutilation of the men.

"The Doniphan boy!" C.B. Wilder shrieked as he leapt from the saddle and stumbled crazily in the snow close to where O'Keefe and Angel North stood. He fell down hard, sprawling full length.

The priest and his woman wrenched their staring eyes away from the blood-spattered corpses of Groves and French, frightened by the intrusion of Wilder. Then they saw who he was and became calm.

Until another revolver shot exploded and the Bar-M foreman was inert in the wedge of light pointing out from the open doorway. The bullet had drilled through the crown of his hat and through his skull into his brain.

The priest had to bring his eyes and his gun to bear on the target now. This time it was the mechanics of guns that acted in his favor. His was already cocked after killing Ralph Doniphan. The ferryman's wife had to use time in thumbling back the hammer of her weapon.

"Evil!—" was her dying word as O'Keefe's Colt exploded another killing shot.

Edge heard the voice and the report. The new death occurred inside the house, out of his sight. And he saw only the killer and his woman on the periphery of his vision, his eyes focusing upon the square of light at the shattered window beyond them. The narrow slits of blue glinted as dangerously as the shards of glass still clinging in the frame.

The head and shoulders of a man showed at the window, dark and featureless against the light from behind. The obscene length of a double-barreled shotgun protruded from the shadowy figure. Light from the lamp and from the moon showed in stark detail the twin hammers, cocked. The trigger guard. The white finger curled close to the point of tipping the hammers.

Edge was the target.

He drew, cocked, leveled, and fired the Remington. The bullet hissed through the river spray and exploded crimson droplets from the flesh at the center of the man's forehead. His head snapped back from the neck. His hands released the shotgun, which bounced off the window frame and dropped to the snow outside.

The third member of the Doniphan family to die on this eve of evil dropped out of sight.

As he holstered the revolver, Edge noticed for the first time the brightly colored paper and sparkling tinsel decorations, which trimmed the walls of the lighted rooms. And he thought fleetingly of the farmstead in Iowa at Christmastime. When Jamie and he had spent hours in the making and hanging of similar festive bunting.

"Have no regret, sir!" O'Keefe urged as he replaced his hat after fixing the gun inside—and misunderstood the reason for the frown on the half-breed's lean, bristled face. "We are soldiers in the army of the Lord. Come the dawn of the new day and all our actions will be seen to be justified."

Both he and Angel North upturned their faces to the moon and starlit sky. And the depth of their genuine belief in O'Keefe's words was plain to see.

Edge shifted his unblinking gaze away from them toward the swollen, rushing river. "Soldiering I'm good at," he drawled cheerlessly as his eyes became baleful. "But a sailor I got no wish to be—especially on this Christmastide."

Chapter Nine

ONCE, during the war, he had briefly captained a stolen Confederate ironclad down the James River in Virginia. The waters had been calm. More recently he had traveled as a passenger aboard a Missouri sternwheeler thrashing northward from Omaha. The surface of that river had been smooth enough to freeze over in South Dakota.

Inevitably, violence had played a bloody part on both trips. This he had accepted without attaching any blame to being waterborne. It was a crossing of San Francisco Bay in a tiny rowboat that had developed his aversion to being away from dry land.

But this new experience was worse than that. Out in California he had been able to burden the responsibility for his fate on the skillful shoulders of a reluctant boatman who knew the deep, salt waters of the bay. While he had withdrawn into a private world of insulating thought—been almost oblivious to the dangers of drowning until the crossing was over and he viewed it in retrospect.

This night it was left to him to handle the long, broad beamed, flat-bottomed mackinaw—after the others had helped to push and drag it down to the rushing water and launch it out into the violent currents. For, after leaping aboard, they huddled together on a center seat and clung to the gunwales at either side, trusting in God, the strength of their grip and, perhaps, the ability of the half-breed to get them to the far bank.

Cursing through clenched teeth, his eyes cracked to the merest slivers of icy blue against the stinging spume, Edge could control nothing except the rudder, his feet braced against lockers and both hands fisted around the tiller.

But even had the stunted, rotund priest and the full-bodied women taken up the oars, they would probably have had little effect on the progress of the mackinaw. For the rushing, resentful, viciously malevolent river claimed and treated the boat as another piece of bankside debris—tossing and pitching it like a chunk of driftwood.

For what seemed an eternity of stretched seconds, the tall, lean half-breed surrendered to the encroachment of the ice of fear that spread from the pit of his stomach to engulf his entire body. But then he summoned up the experiences of a lifetime to conquer the terror. His lifetime, what was left of it, was as his sole possession and now he saw the ugliness of the flooding river as just one more evil challenge from the ruling fate that sought to rob him of everything.

The initial thrust of the bows into the water was almost immediately negated by the powerful sweep of the rushing water. Inky blackness thudded against the hull and became a million drops of icy whiteness spraying over the side, lashing the three figures and merging again as a bubbled swill around their feet.

The bows came about and would have smashed into the grassy bank from which the mackinaw had been launched had not Edge held the rudder hard over. Instead, it was rushed downriver at the dictate of the flood.

The priest and the woman had their backs to the half-breed. They were shouting. But not to him. Above the crash of water and creak of timbers, he heard disjointed words and phrases. O'Keefe was praying at the top of his voice. Angel North interjected countless Amens.

The boat was surrendered by one current to another. Edge, his face streaming with water, acted instinctively to reposition the rudder. But he had no way of knowing whether this had any effect on the diagonal course of the mackinaw out into midstream. More drenching water broke over the gunwale to slop along the bottom of the boat.

The single light in the town of Fallon was now behind him. So was the moon. There were just the white slopes of the valley on either side. The star patterned sky above. And the raging river beneath. Droplets of spray clung to his eyelashes, blurring his vision and making it even more difficult to keep his bearings.

He recalled his pathetically lame excuse for taking the night ride to Fallon—the near-empty tobacco poke. This thought sparked self-anger, which blocked any reasoned consideration of why he had elected to join O'Keefe and the woman aboard the flood-tossed boat.

Then it was over. With a suddenness that sprang the word "miraculous" into his mind. He saw ahead what seemed to be an impenetrable wall of solid blackness against the snow. A powerful current rushed the boat toward it and there was no response from the rudder. The craft was turned sideways-on, as if at the start of an uncontrollable spin. The low boughs of a tree slapped across the half-breed's face, spattering him with the wet of melted snow.

The mackinaw did do a complete turnabout, but slowly. And the pitching motion was almost halted. It was being propelled by its own momentum across a small lagoon encircled by timber.

The priest curtailed his prayer.

Angel North stood erect and gazed around in wonder. "We are saved, Father!" she gasped.

"Do not sound surprised, daughter," O'Keefe said calmly. "It is God's will."

"Best you wait until we're ashore to thank Him," Edge growled. "I'm told shipboard romances don't last."

He licked the water from his thin lips and tasted salt. He realized it was the sweat of fear that had opened his pores.

"Do not conceal your faith, sir!" O'Keefe chided. "You have it, or why else did you cross with daughter and me?"

"I don't know," the half-breed replied as he picked up his Winchester from the deep water in the bottom of the boat. "It even seemed a lousy idea at the time."

The lagoon's opening to the river was some twenty feet wide. The flood water continued to rush by but its angry roar was less loud now, the sound strangely absorbed by the surrounding trees. The boat grounded with a gentle thud on a snow-covered shingle beach.

O'Keefe and Angel North hauled the bow of the mackinaw high out of the water as Edge started through the trees, the beacon light of the Fallon Hotel gleaming among the evergreen foliage to show him the way to take.

The diagonal crossing of Wind River had carried the mackinaw a half mile downstream and Edge had covered almost half the distance back again before a glance over his shoulder showed him the priest and the woman emerging from the trees.

"At least two people are having a good time this Christmas," he muttered.

He stayed close to the river all the way to the point immediately opposite the Doniphan house. Lamplight continued to shine from two windows and the open door. The horses had wandered a little, but not far. The bodies of Wilder, Groves, and French looked from this distance like abandoned sacks of something unspecific.

On this side of the river there was a broad jetty, which sometimes showed above the surface and was a moment later awash. A much larger ferryboat than the mackinaw was moored by six lines to the downstream side of the jetty. The ropes were rigidly taut under the strain of holding the boat against the powerful challenge of the river. It was a purpose-built craft with low sides and a bow and stern in the form of long ramps at present in the raised position. It was large enough to carry a wagon and four-horse team. It creaked and shuddered and the ropes that held it groaned.

After a glance toward the light in Fallon and another back at the couple hurrying through the snow, Edge was gripped by an unreasonable compulsion to draw the razor from his neck pouch and saw through the ferryboat's mooring lines.

But he spat forcefully into the dark, white spume-scarred river, having decided he had done enough unreasonable things for one day. And started up the steep slope to town.

The temperature had dropped again and when he moved off the trail from the ferry and onto the street, he heard no dripping of melted snow from the eaves of the buildings. The only sounds were made by the distant river and his footfalls in the snow. Until he reached the square formed by the intersection of two streets where the Fallon Hotel was sited. Then a clock, higher up in the town, began to chime the hour of midnight. Higher still, on the snow-capped ridge above Fallon, a wolf howled.

The windows of the hotel were dimly lit in contrast to the bright lamp illuminating the wooden sign. And were misted with condensation. When the double, one-piece wooden doors were pushed open, a little more light spilled out to fall across Edge.

Two men stood swaying on the threshold, each with an arm hanging around the shoulder of the other. They had sweat-sheened, liquor-reddened faces. And each had a brimful shot glass in his free hand. They grinned foolishly at the half-breed, drunkenly friendly.

"Hey, hear that, mister?" one of them invited.

"Means it's Christmas day," the other added. They both lifted their glasses and emptied them down throats immune to the searing effect of the whiskey. "You wouldn't by any chance be Santa Claus?"

"No, Fred. He ain't gotta sack."

"Looking for one to climb into is all," Edge answered as the clock finished chiming and the wolf ceased its anguished howling.

"Come along inside, stranger!" a third man invited, friendly without being drunk. "This is the place you been lookin' for."

Edge stepped up on to the stoop.

"Big night, Jethro!" the elder of the two celebrating old-timers announced after peering across the intersection. "Two more folks acomin' up the hill." He lowered his voice. "Sad, ain't it, George?"

"What is, Fred?"

"Folks bein' far from home at Christmas? Away from their loved ones and all?"

"Hey, Fred?"

"Yeah, George?"

"What's with Ralph and Emily Doniphan tonight? All them lights on in the house at this hour?"

Edge glanced down the hill and across the river just before he entered the hotel. The horses were gone from sight now, perhaps around to the blind side of the house. The dark humps in the snow were even more difficult to recognize from this distance.

"Does it matter, George?"

"No, Fred. Not to us."

"Then let's have another drink."

"Sure thing, Fred."

The saloon section of the Fallon Hotel was well appointed by frontier standards. It was a square room with a bar counter running halfway along the rear and a side wall. The counter was of polished timber and the walls were whitened and hung with badly executed oil paintings in gilt frames. The tables and chairs were in the same style as the L-shaped bar. In one corner were gaming tables for cards, roulette, and craps. Plus a wheel of fortune. In another was a semi-circular stage fringed with velvet drapes.

The middle-aged, brightly smiling man behind the bar looked as neat and clean as the bottles and glasses arranged on the shelves behind him. The two old-timers, their Sunday-best suits a little rumpled and stained by the drinking session, had been the only patrons before Edge entered. They returned now to the table nearest an ornate stove, which had filled the saloon with pleasant heat before they opened the doors.

Light was supplied by only four of the many lamps that hung around the walls.

"Only got us two boarding guests right now, sir," the bartender said as Edge moved up to the bar in front of him and rested the Winchester stock on the floor, the barrel leaning against his leg. "So you and your friends almost got the pick of the hotel rooms."

"Friends?" Edge said, and added: "Whiskey."

With the dexterity of a man proud of his craft, the bartender swung a bottle and a shot glass from a shelf behind him to the countertop in front of him. "They said two others were coming." He looked toward the open doorway, which was admitting the cold night air. "I thought that as you reached Fallon more or less at the same time . . ."

Edge uncorked the bottle and poured liquor into the

glass. "I know them," he allowed, and swallowed the slug of whiskey in one gulp.

The old men at the table by the stove were drinking slowly now, savoring the last drainings from the bottle that stood empty between them. They blew out fresh cigar smoke, which served to mask the staleness of the old that permeated the atmosphere.

The bartender's smile continued to expose his teeth and form the line of his lips. But his eyes showed anxiety. "There won't be any trouble, sir?"

"Seems that depends upon the Almighty," the half-breed replied, doing nothing to sooth the other man's unease. Then he delved into his hip pocket and produced a five dollar bill, which he placed on the bartop. "For the drink and in advance for the room, feller. Be obliged if you'd tell me where to find the room. The closest one will be fine."

The bartender blinked several times. Then cleared his throat and nodded toward a door at the end of the bar section running along the rear wall. "Through there and up the stairway, Mr. . . ."

"Edge."

"Yes, well. Up the stairs like I say. Any room except number ten. That's the bridal suite and we . . . yes, well." He cleared his throat again. "You're wet through, Mr. Edge. If you'd like to leave your clothes outside your door, I'll bring them down to dry by the stove. I'll be closin' up pretty soon. Then I have to decorate the saloon for tomorrow and—"

"Obliged, feller," the half-breed interrupted as the footfalls of O'Keefe and Angel North sounded on the stoop boarding outside. He showed a quiet smile as he picked up his rifle. "But it ain't my birthday. And that's the only suit I got apart from these clothes."

"Sir!" the priest called excitedly as he escorted the woman into the saloon. "Please tell daughter and I that we have reached the end of our search?"

The old timers got hurriedly to their feet. They bowed unsteadily.

"Howdy, ma'am," Fred greeted.

"And a Merry Christmas to you, lady," George added.

Angel's radiant smile rewarded them and still had ample warmth to spare for the nervous and bemused Jethro behind the bar.

"I'm sorry?"

"Please, a woman with child named Mary and her husband Joseph?" O'Keefe implored, his voice tremulous with avid expectation.

"Oh, yeah. We got Maria Lass—"

Edge closed the door behind him on the warm, dimly lit, smoke-reeking saloon. And heard nothing more of the exchange except a squeal of delight from the one-time Virginia City whore.

Enough moonglow and the reflection of its blue light off snow filtered through windows to show him the way up the staircase and reveal halls leading off the landing at the top. Nine of the doors flanking the landings stood ajar and he pushed open the one bearing the number two.

It was functionally comfortable, furnished with a single bed, a chair, a bureau, and a closet to hang clothes. There was a strip of rush matting beside the bed. Small framed prints were fixed to the whitened walls. A window overlooked the square in front of the hotel.

The air was cold and free of odor, except that of being unused for a long time. No sounds intruded from outside.

There was a pitcher of water in a bowl on the dresser and a towel folded beside it. After he had stripped off all his clothing, Edge ignored the water but used the towel to rub dryness and warmth into the flesh of his bullet-scarred body. Then he hung his damp clothing in the closet and climbed in under the clean blankets. The bristles of his face rasped on the crisp fabric of the pillow. The wood and metal of the Winchester stayed cold for a long time in the bed. He slept his shallow, energy-restoring sleep with his right hand fisted around the frame of the rifle.

But there was no risk of him putting a bullet into the full, ripe body of Angel North when she stepped into the room, unless his subconscious defensive mechanism had warned him the woman posed a threat.

He heard the click of the door latch and sprang open his eyes. The narrowest, brightest blue threads against a background of dark hues, dark brown skin and jet black bristles.

Brilliant sunlight streamed in through the window, entering at a low angle to show that the day was still very young. Edge did not blink in response to it as he shifted his eyes to the full extent in their sockets without moving his head. The door swung open noiselessly on well-oiled hinges and the woman moved across the threshold. She looked much as she had when he last saw her, except that the semi-circles of creased shadows under her brown eyes were much darker. Her hands were at her sides and empty.

"I know it's Christmas," he said evenly, and the words froze her into immobility and spurred a gasp from her full lips. "But you ain't my idea of God's gift to mankind, ma'am."

She recovered quickly from the surprise. The momentary fear was gone from her once-beautiful face and the former expression of nervous tension took command of her features.

"Please, I beg of you? There may be trouble. Father has asked if you will help us."

The half-breed had sat upright, his back against the head of the bed so that the blankets fell away from him, revealing his naked torso to the base of his flat belly. She was a one-time whore and he knew it. He did not expect, and she did not show, any embarrassment. Nor interest in the muscular, dark-toned body with its matting of black hair on the chest and the livid, dead tissue that were the signs of old bullet wounds at his left shoulder, right hip, and just below the elbow on the inside of his left arm.

"How'd I get to owe you two anything?" he asked, and threw off the bedcovers to swing his bare feet to the rush matting.

The woman's expression did not alter as he stood up and moved to the closet, revealing his total nakedness. She made no point of not looking at any particular part of him. It was as if he were fully clothed.

"Not us, mister. The world!"

"That ain't done nothing for me either, lady," Edge growled, grimacing at the stiff, cold, still damp touch of the red longjohns against his flesh.

"Money!" Angel North sneered. "You want money?"

"Not right now. Got enough for my needs." He pulled on his pants. "What kind of trouble?"

The question was impulsive, to such an extent that for part of a second he did not believe he had asked it. The woman spoke eagerly across the start of his self-anger.

"Maria Lassiter wants to get to her dad before he dies. But she's near to her time. The local doctor says she can't travel. And because of that Redeker won't give us the okay."

The air in the small room had been fugged with the effects of Edge's sleeping. With the door open the atmosphere had freshened and now seemed to be laden with invisible icicles that jabbed their points into his flesh. He glanced out of the window and saw that the sky was almost solid blue, marred only by the yellow ball of the rising sun. The snow sparkled with an overlay of frost crystals. The section of the Wind River he could see was still at a high level, but it flowed slow and smooth with no whitecaps to disturb the surface.

"Can't O'Keefe handle killing them himself?" the half-breed asked as he finished buttoning his shirt.

She crossed the room and, close up, he saw the depth of her fatigue inscribed on the sallow skin of her face. And smelt the staleness of her body, which had been too long in the same clothes. She thrust up the window and a new invasion of clean, ice-cold air dispelled the smell of her.

"Take a look, mister," she invited.

Edge buckled on his gunbelt and tied the holster down to his thigh as he pushed his head and shoulders out of the open window.

The snow on the streets had been trampled by many feet. Immediately below three men stood in front of the hotel stoop, wrapped in warm clothing and holding rifles. Higher up the broad main street of Fallon, a group of people were filing into the church. Countless footprints in the frost-crisped snow indicated that many other worshippers had preceded them.

Above and to the right of the window the lamp that illuminated the hotel sign glimmered ineffectually in the morning sun. It was impossible to see if the lights in the Doniphan house over the river were still on. The frozen corpses of the Bar-M hands were veiled by the dazzle from water and snow.

Edge withdrew his head and closed the window. "Lots of people go to church at Christmas," he said as he shrugged into his topcoat, put on his hat and carried his boots over to the bed. "What kind of service are the three fellers down below giving?"

"We told the men in the saloon last night about all the signs of the second coming," Angel North said quickly. "We demanded to see Mary . . . Maria. The bartender wouldn't let us. He held a scattergun on us.

Sent the drunks out to fetch some people. The sheriff and the doctor and the local preacher. But they told others. The saloon was crowded. We been talkin' and arguin' all night. You must've heard the noise?"

"Would have if it had been any business of mine," Edge answered.

The woman showed brief confusion at this, then shrugged it off as irrelevant. "Anyway, this town is filled with people who have faith, mister. Our message of the signs has been received in the manner we give it. Almost everyone in Fallon believes Jesus Christ is to be born again."

She savored the triumph of this achievement as Edge lifted the Winchester from the bed and canted it to his left shoulder.

"There was a lot of trouble the first time around," the half-breed said flatly. "So what—"

The moment of relief from anxiety was quickly passed, dispelled by the half-breed's reference to her reason for coming to his room.

"They want it to be here in their town!" Angel North answered quickly. "But it cannot be. You can see that, can't you, mister? All the signs so far show it should be like it was before. The stable and the shepherds . . ." She paused, bewildered, then shook her head. "In a different country half a world away, maybe . . . but not here in Fallon! In a hotel! With a lot of the people only fakin' faith. Really just want it to be here so the town'll be famous and lots of folks will come and bring money and . . ."

If Edge had ever had doubts about the woman's motives, they would have been negated now. The tears that flowed from her eyes and the degree of anguish inscribed upon her face were obviously triggered by some deep-seated feeling completely devoid of materialistic desires. Her despair was as genuine as the other extreme of emotion that had in the past allowed her sallow, exhausted, hard-used face to express radiance.

"Please!" She dropped to her knees in front of him and interlocked her fingers under the point of her chin. Her eyes as she upturned her face toward him were suddenly like those of a young child begging for mercy from a source of terror. "Please, mister, at least try to help us?"

She unfastened her hands and tipped them palms upwards, extending her arms out in front of her. "Please," she whispered.

"Some might say you've come to the last feller in the world to help you, lady," he said flatly, eyeing the supplicating woman with cold-eyed disrelish. "But I guess beggers can't be choosers."

Chapter Ten

SHE led him out of the room, across the landing and along the hallway on the other side. The door to room ten was still the only one firmly closed. She opened it without knocking and stepped across the threshold.

"Here, Father," she said, her initial excitement at Edge's bald agreement to help already diminished. "It was all I could think of."

The room was larger than the one the half-breed had chosen but was furnished in a similar style. Except that the bed was double size and there were two of everything else. And it was heated by a portable oil stove that tained the air with its fumes.

The blonde, pale-faced Maria Lassiter lay in the center of the big bed. The Mexican-looking father of her unborn child sat on a chair at one side, holding her right hand in both of his. A tall, thin, recently shaved and talced man with an ill-tempered expression had claimed the second chair on the other side of the bed. A black valise at his feet marked him as the doctor, but he had the kind of features that had probably made him look like an undertaker as soon as he was old enough for his face to hint at his character. He was now in his early sixties.

O'Keefe was kneeling at the foot of the bed and it was impossible to tell whether he had been praying to the Almighty or making entreaties to the mortal when the newcomers interrupted him.

The sheriff was by the double window, which looked out over the street. He was middle-aged and compactly built, with a handlebar moustache and ears that stuck out to an almost comical extent. He was fully dressed for the weather outside, unlike the others, except that the priest still wore his hat. And he was fully prepared for trouble. His hands were draped over the butts of the matched Colts jutting from the holster at each hip.

"You!" the pregnant girl gasped.

"Mr. Edge?" Redeker exclaimed.

"Really!" the doctor complained with an effeminate stamp of his foot.

"What the hell?" the lawman demanded.

"It is no use, daughter," O'Keefe groaned.

Only Joe Redeker extended some kind of warmth toward the half-breed.

"Happy Christmas," Edge said wryly. "Sometimes the impossible happens."

"He's the man who's seen all the signs we have," Angel North told the sheriff.

Edge ignored the others as he found his gaze trapped by the stare from Maria's big brown eyes. The emnity they had first showed was abruptly replaced by something else. Not friendliness, or even disdain. Instead they expressed the same kind of pleading the former whore had directed at him a few moments before.

"This young lady must not be moved from this bed!" the doctor proclaimed. "I have forbidden it!"

Nobody listened.

"You've seen my father?" Maria asked.

"Last night."

"He's dying?" She did not look as if she even hoped for a negative reply.

"Had a stroke, I figure. Can't move a muscle below his neck. Now can't talk."

The girl pulled out of Redeker's grip, fisted both her

hands and thudded them against her temples. "I must go to him!" she wailed.

"I'm sorry, my dear girl," the doctor said consolingly. "But I must insist. Not only for the sake of your baby. But your own life will be in danger if—"

"It's gonna come early, Mr. Edge," Redeker explained, and his interruption made the doctor look even more ill-tempered. "Not in another two weeks like we figured at first. Must have been the long trip, or maybe what happened with them two Bar-M hands yesterday mornin'. Whatever, Doc Tatum here says it could happen any minute."

"Clear them out of here, Mr. Karnes!" Doctor Tatum ordered shrilly. "Everyone except the father-to-be! The mother must not be excited!"

"Stay where you are, sir!"

Edge and Angel North were the only people in the room behind O'Keefe. And had seen him take off his hat as the commanding tone of the doctor's voice captured attention. As the pudgy hand was raised to the brim of the hat, the one time whore had caught her breath and shot a desperate look at Edge. The half-breed said and did nothing.

"Mary wishes it!" O'Keefe said softly as he covered the lawman with his Colt and his eyes but sensed others watching him.

"Maria, mister!" Redeker snapped. "You been talkin' crazy about—"

The girl in the bed lowered her fists, calmness replacing anguish. "It isn't important, Joe," she cut in. "The reason they want to take me isn't important. Just so long as I get to Dad's side."

"Edge!" Sheriff Karnes growled, looking even more comical now with his arms held away from his sides like half-opened wings. "You ain't the kinda man to get took by this crazy religious nonsense?"

"It's not important!" Maria said, her tone as earnest

as her expression as she looked along the length of the bed and past the fat little priest at the impassive, unmoving half breed. "It doesn't matter! That part of it! If you help me get to my father . . ." She searched in the turmoil of her mind for something that would spur the tall, lean, unshaven man out of his inaction. "If he's going to die as you say, I'll inherit the Bar-M. I'll be able to pay anything you demand!"

"It could cost you your life, my dear girl!" Tatum threatened, exasperated.

"I don't care!" Maria flung back at him.

Edge arced the Winchester down from his shoulder to smack the barrel into the waiting cup of his free hand. "Raise them higher, sheriff," he instructed flatly. "No sense in more than one life being on the line."

"Two!" the doctor growled. "She is with child."

"Two makes it surer, Doc," the half-breed replied. "If somebody wants something that bad, they deserve the chance."

"Your kind ain't that kind!" the lawman snarled. "You gotta have an angle!"

"Maybe it's a right one for once," Edge answered.

"Daughter, the sheriff's guns!" O'Keefe instructed, the excitement as he got a foretaste of triumph putting a shrill note into his voice.

Angel North complied with the order, taking care to stay out of the firing line.

"Mr. Edge," Redeker groaned, white-faced and impotent on the chair. "Maria doesn't know what she's sayin'. She don't realize what might happen if—"

"Joe!" the girl carrying his child snapped. Then moderated her tone as she saw the depth of his anguish. "Yesterday morning you said how beholden you were to him. All of us might have been dead already if he had not helped. Now's your chance to repay him. Get my clothes from the closet, darling."

"No debt owed, feller," Edge corrected. "Just your girl asking for a favor."

Meekly, afraid and uncomprehending, Redeker rose from the chair and moved toward the closets.

"How you figure to get by my deputies outside?" the lawman sneered. "Any shootin' and all the folks in church'll come runnin'. And most of 'em are hooked on all this holy crap the priest's been spoutin'."

"The Almighty will provide the inspiration," O'Keefe said confidently.

"Outside in the hallway, if you please," Maria Lassiter said, entirely composed. "While I dress."

It was fifteen minutes later, as the clock in the higher part of town struck the single note of six-thirty, when the trio of deputies swung their heads and their rifles toward the sound of horses hooves and buggy wheels crunching through the snow.

The roofed cut-under, which had brought Maria Lassiter and Joseph Redeker to Fallon, came around the corner of the cross street that ran along the side of the hotel. The pregnant girl, her legs and swollen belly draped by the blanket, had control of the reins. Edge sat on the padded seat beside her and there was nothing false about the expression of sheer terror that contorted her wan face. It was as real as the threat of the straight razor which the half-breed held close to her pulsing throat.

For though she had agreed to the subterfuge it was with keen misgivings. She did not trust the changed attitude of the taciturn man at her side. Yesterday she had seen him kill without compunction. And now he was risking his life to help her, apparently convinced to do so simply because she was prepared to risk her own. So she feared some evil trick that would result in the honed blade of the razor slicing deep into her flesh.

Doctor Tatum and Sheriff Karnes walked beside the buggy, slowly, as if they were already accompanying a funeral hearse. Behind them were O'Keefe with his Colt trained on the lawman's back and Joe Redeker who covered the doctor with Edge's Winchester. Angel North was on the other side, with one hand on the bridle of the gelding pulling the buggy.

"Take it easy," Karnes said tensely as the three surprised deputies found targets for their rifles. "Drop them guns and walk on down to the ferry ahead of us."

"What goes on, Deke?"

"What the hell does it matter?" the sheriff snarled as the buggy and escort continued to close in on the guards. "Nothin' is worth anybody get killed over! Do like I tell you!"

The deputies looked at each other, back at the buggy, then flung their rifles into the snow and started down the hill. For the first few yards they kept glancing back over their shoulders, as if trying to convince themselves that they had really seen the hostages and captors. But after that they stared fixedly ahead.

"Why'd you post the guards, sheriff?" Edge asked conversationally. He glanced to left and right, checking on the blank facades of the buildings flanking the broad street. And out through the rear window of the buggy toward the church up the hill.

"Town council decision," Karnes growled.

"Of which I am chief executive," Tatum said officiously. "Premature births are always difficult. And this one will be even more difficult now. The guards were placed on the hotel to keep the religious fanatics and the curious away. Miss Lassiter should not be excited."

"Will we reach the place where her pa is before her time, Doc?" Redecker asked.

In stark contrast with the smile of confidence on the face of O'Keefe walking beside him, the young father-to-be wore a tormented expression of deep anxiety. It seemed to take an enormous effort for him to keep the Winchester leveled at Tatum's narrow back.

"That is in God's hands, I'm afraid," the doctor replied dully.

"Which means there is no need to be afraid, brothers," the priest advised, his voice resonant with true belief. "He will ensure that His Son is born at the appointed place."

"Amen!" Angel North intoned.

"Nonsense," Maria Lassiter rasped softly, her mind eased a little now that the difficulty of the deputies had been overcome. "You surely do not believe in any of this, do you, Edge?"

"No, ma'am," he answered. "Maybe on account of I haven't come across even one wise man yet."

"You don't consider yourself wise?" she posed wryly.

"No, ma'am," he replied as the buggy reached the foot of the slope and Angel North halted the gelding at the jetty. "If I was that I wouldn't be down here. Be up in town at whatever store sells tobacco."

Close to, the Wind River had a menacing look. Dark with silt and sheened by the sun, the fast flowing but calm surface of the water emanated a brand of malevolent evil that boded a greater danger than when it had been in full, raging flood. The river's power was still evident from the slanting tautness of the lines which restrained the ferryboat close to the jetty.

Everyone saw this, but only the four lawmen, the doctor, and Joe Redeker eyed the water with unease. Maria's anxiety was founded on the illness of her father. Edge watched the church up the hill. Angel North was in a cocoon of serenity woven by her faith.

O'Keefe issued instructions in a firm voice, his bristled, fatigue-drawn face expressing a smile of quiet confidence.

All but one of the mooring lines was unhitched. It was the rope to the stern that remained fixed, so that the downstream currents swung the ferry into a quarter turn, pushing the bow toward the bank.

Maria Lassiter was the only hostage under threat of instant death now, for the combined strength of all the men except Edge was required to drag the high-riding ferry up against the jetty and to hitch the shortened line around the cleat. Then Redeker clambered aboard to lower the stern ramp.

The gelding in the shafts of the buggy was nervously aware of the river's malevolence. But Angel North spoke soft words of comfort into a pricked ear of the animal as she tugged gently on the bridle. Her voice was the only one to be heard, for she was the only person down by the river with need to speak. Everybody else thought his or her own thoughts.

Up in the town church, a pump organ began to play. And a mass of voices were raised in the singing of "Rock of Ages."

The cut-under buggy came to a halt on the gently rocking ferry. The men who were cooperating with morose reluctance could no longer see Maria Lassiter and the blade held close to her throat. But the face of Edge was framed in the glass window at the rear of the buggy. And it was the very lack of any expression on the dark-hued features—the utter coldness of the slitted blue eyes—which caused the men to abandon any counter moves they may have been considering.

Redeker did not attempt to reclaim the half-breed's Winchester from where he had rested it on the buggy's footboard. The priest, surrounded by the three deputies, Karnes, and Tatum on the jetty, did not reach for the Colt that he had put back inside his hat before lending a hand with the rope.

The face of Edge was enough encouragement for the men to comply with the request: "We need all of you to help with the crossing, brothers."

They came aboard as a group, no one man taking the lead.

"It's the kid I can't understand, Deke," one of the deputies growled as they watched Redeker haul up the ramp. "How come he had a gun in his hands instead of in his back?"

"It was only me and the doc that would have been killed, Frank," Karnes growled. "The guy with the razor reckoned he wouldn't have killed the girl. But her and Redeker didn't trust him."

"All that doesn't matter now," Maria said shrilly as the half-breed stepped down from the buggy, the razor back in the pouch and the Winchester canted to his left shoulder. "Please get us to the other side."

"Yes, that is what we must do!" O'Keefe urged. "After the child is born today, such evils as threats and distrust and hatred will have no place in the world. The sins which prevailed even after the first coming of our—"

"Best you keep the sermon for another time and another place, feller," Edge called from the position he had taken at the stern after Redeker had moved to the buggy. "Unless you figure you can top the one already given by the Fallon preacher."

O'Keefe had been temporarily detached from his immediate surroundings and their dangers as he launched into his oration. He was bewildered by his sudden return to reality. But he resumed command of himself and the others with composed speed.

"They're coming from church? Please cast us off from the shore, brother. Everyone to the poles."

For stretched seconds there was dignified peace and tranquility in front of Fallon's church as the early-morning congregation emerged from the arched doorway. But then somebody noted the absence of the three guards from their sentry positions outside the hotel. Suspicion was aroused and spread. Many eyes directed their gaze toward the tracks in the snow left by the buggy and its walking escorts. The volume of talk rose, the tones shrill or hoarse, as the sign drew every eye down to the river and the jetty. In time to see that the ferry was broadside on to the bank just before a sun-glinting metal blade sliced through the final mooring line.

And the craft lunged forward in the triumphant grip of the river currents.

The congregation was spurred into equally sudden movement then, abruptly became an enraged mob that slithered and stumbled down the treacherous, snow-covered slope of the street. Doomed to fail but refusing to acknowledge failure. Men and women of all ages. And children. In the grip of religious fervor or driven by the anger of material loss. Wailing, sobbing, screaming, and cursing.

Aboard the ferry the noise of the mob was heard. But no one looked toward the mass advance. For the river was once more the prime enemy, in reckless control of the heavy, lumbering craft.

Today there was no violent pitching or rolling, no spray breaking over the sides to threaten those on board with imminent death from drowning in the ice cold water. Now the danger was from the ferry being snatched by some powerful undertow, perhaps to be borne downstream for miles, perhaps for just a few yards, before a stronger counter current took command and dashed it into a bank. The bottom could be ripped open by a snag. Or the angle of impact could capsize the ungainly craft.

The only defense against such a disaster was the brute strength the men could apply to three poles, concentrating all their efforts on the port side to force the ferry across the thrust of the currents.

The danger common to all negated the emnity of those who had come abroad under duress toward those who had been the captors. So that Edge, Tatum, and O'Keefe worked at their pole with as much strength as each was able to muster. Redeker and one of the deputies were on another pole. And the sheriff and two remaining lawmen applied their weight and strength to the third.

Maria Lassiter sat fearfully in the buggy, tightly gripping the padded seat as the restless movements of the gelding rocked and jolted the vehicle. The unafraid Angel North continued to speak placating words to the animal.

The men were grouped at the bow of the craft, thrusting the poles hard into the river bed, not so much concerned with propelling the ferry forward as to keep her headed out toward midstream. And, as had happened with the much smaller, lighter boat last night, this one followed a lengthy but inexorable course diagonally from one bank toward the other.

At first the men cursed—at the poles, the ferry, and the river. But soon the only sounds to be forced from between their clenched teeth were grunts and gasps, as the sweat beads of exertion coursed their flesh and they called upon the willpower of their minds to supplement the strength of their bodies.

Behind them, the citizens of Fallon moved along the east bank of the Wind River. Silent now as the widening gap of water emphasized their impotence. Whether they wanted the ferry to flounder and sink or to safely reach the opposite bank perhaps even they themselves did not know.

Ahead of the lumbering craft and the men struggling to control its direction, three riders steered their horses along the west bank—men and mounts briefly glimpsed because there was no time to devote to anything that was happening outside of the existence of the ferry on the river.

Until one of the horsemen whirled his right hand in

the air above his head. And the loop of a lariat curled over the starboard gunwale and slapped against the deck.

Perhaps everyone aboard saw this. But all with the exception of Edge considered the task of the moment too important to abandon it.

The half-breed released his grip on the pole and lunged across the deck. Tatum cursed and O'Keefe howled in dismay as the strength of the most powerful man was abruptly lost. The pole was sunk deep into the river bed and they could not wrench it free before the ferry swung, and the two remaining men had to leave go or be dragged overboard.

The diving form of Edge spooked the gelding into a rear and Angel North was sent stumbling backwards. She and Maria screamed. The lawmen and Redeker struggled to bring the ferry back on to its cross-current course.

Edge was down on his belly, his arms at full stretch to hook his clawed fingers over the lariat loop. As the swinging action of the boat drew the rope taut and he was dragged across the deck, he cursed. His anger was directed inwardly again, triggered by the realization of another uncharacteristic lapse of his ability to anticipate danger. He had taken part in shoving off the boat from one bank without considering the even more difficult task of docking it against the other.

No more rope was played out from the shore and the half-breed was jerked hard into the angle of the bow ramp and side of the ferry. The pain of the impact augmented what he was already suffering from his dive to the deck. The honda hissed around the loop and trapped both his hands. It felt as if his arms were within a fraction of an inch of being wrenched from their sockets.

Then footfalls thudded on the deck behind him. And the bright blueness of the sky was blotted out as men leaned over him, to fist the rope in their hands. He heard their grunts as they called upon their diminished strength in a renewed fight against the river.

The gelding snorted and scraped hooves against the deck.

"We're saved! We're saved! Praise the Lord!" The voice was Angel North's, shrilling to a high soprano pitch.

With the others taking the strain of the rope, there was enough slack behind them for Edge to pull his hands out of the loop and get to his feet. Every muscle in his body seemed to be burning with the flames of pain. But he was no stranger to suffering of any kind and he was able to fight the urge to sit down and indulge the need for comforting rest.

The gelding was still afraid, ears pricked and eyes bulged. Angel North had re-established a hold on the bridle but was otherwise ignoring the animal as she gazed skyward, radiantly smiling her gratitude. Maria Lassiter was staring at the west bank of the Wind River, incredulity superimposed on the frown of fear.

"It's not possible," she gasped as Edge reclaimed his Winchester from the buggy. "Not my baby!"

Edge snapped his head around to see what had caused the change in the pregnant girl. But he saw just the snow-covered meadow, for the ferry was now bow-on to the bank and the raised ramp concealed the men on the shore. Then the craft shuddered as the impact of the docking was transmitted down its length. And again those with work to do had no time to waste.

While the other men continued to grip the rope, holding the bow of the ferry hard against the bank, Redeker ran to the ramp release latch on one side. Edge went to the other side.

Angel North continued to commune silently with the heavens.

The ramp swung down and crunched into the snow.
"Get the buggy off!" Redeker yelled.

The woman did not hear him. The girl continued to gaze in awe at the shore.

Again the half-breed and the Mexican-looking youngster moved simultaneously, Edge to the left of the gelding and Redeker to the right. They grasped the bridle and yanked at it as they ran forward.

Angel North was knocked to the deck with a cry of alarm as the gelding submitted eagerly to the demands of the two men. Edge, Redeker, the horse, and the buggy thudded and clattered along the deck, down the ramp and onto the snow-draped meadow.

The priest was next to land. Then the other men, Sheriff Karnes half dragging the ex-whore as the ferry, no longer held against the bank, was claimed by the river and dragged out into deep water.

Edge had briefly glimpsed their mounted rescuers, received a fleeting impression of men garbed in strangely bright clothes. For long moment after this, he watched the sheriff, the deputies, the doctor, and Redeker, his reflexes primed to combat any aggressive moves they might make. But exhaustion sank the men to their haunches or caused them to sag against the wheels of the buggy as they panted deep breaths of chill morning air into their punished lungs.

The priest, his woman, and Maria Lassiter stared at the horsemen. The girl was still incredulous. O'Keefe and Angel North expressed a brand of depthless joy that for once appeared to have robbed them of the power of speech.

"Good morning."

"We are happy to have been of some small service."

"Perhaps you are able to assist us. We seek a man named Silas Martin."

Edge heard the monotone, strangely accented voices speaking English and recalled a Burmese poet who had died badly at a mission far to the south. Then he looked at the trio of men who had spoken the words and saw the reason for the joy and disbelief with which others were viewing them.

For the horsemen were Orientals. Men of middle years with yellowish skin and oddly shaped eyes. With their hair plaited into single pigtails and thin, drooping, waxed moustaches. They wore hats shaped like shallow cones and long, silken, multicolored robes belted at the waist. From one side of the belt of each man hung a curved scabbard with the handle of a sword jutting out. To the other side was fastened a conventional holster housing a Colt revolver. They sat astride strong-looking stallions, saddled Western style.

The last man to speak was neatly coiling the lariat, which had been used to hold the ferry boat against the bank.

"Ain't a name I know," the half-breed replied. "Real glad you were looking for him around here. Obliged for the help."

The four lawmen, Joe Redeker, and Doctor Tatum had also recognized the distinctive accents of the mounted men. And now they looked at them in the same manner as Maria Lassiter.

"Hot damn!" the deputy named Frank gasped. "The three from the Orient!"

"We are from the country of Nippon," the man coiling the lariat confirmed, and exchanged puzzled glances with his companions, all three of them suddenly wary of being viewed with awe and disbelief. "Please, can any of you tell us whether Silas Martin is among those on the far side of this river?"

He raised an arm and everyone looked toward the throng on the opposite bank. The bulk of the ferryboat no longer intervened, it was being pushed fast downstream at the mercy of the currents. The people there were silent as they returned the attention of those on the west bank with a higher degree of concentration.

"Ain't nobody of that name lives in Fallon," Sheriff Karnes supplied, trying to shake off the sense of unreality that had gripped him. But there was a huskiness in his voice and as soon as he looked at the trio of horsemen again his gaze was trapped by their alien appearance.

"No, sir. Silas Martin would be visiting. Passing through. He has come from Portland in this country. With a large box."

Karnes shook his head. "Ain't been no strangers in town for at least two months. Until these people came."

He began to nod, indicating individuals in the group around the buggy. But then saw that he had lost the interest of the Orientals.

"We thank you, sir. And again we say we are happy to have helped you. Now we must go. To look for Silas Martin."

"But you can't!" O'Keefe exclaimed, his joy suddenly gone. "You must come with us to the stable!"

The Orientals exchanged more puzzled, wary glances.

"Sir?"

"Jesus Christ is to be born again!" the priest explained quickly. "We have Mary and Joseph. We have the shepherds. We have the Angel. You are the three Kings from the Orient. You must come with us!"

"No!"

"This means nothing to us, sir!"

"We must continue our search for Silas Martin."

The three were no longer wary. And had abandoned their curiosity. Now they were simply impatient to restart their interrupted mission. And they gathered in their reins and tugged on them to turn the horses away from the buggy.

"Edge!" O'Keefe shrieked. And swung both hands up to grip the brim of his hat.

The half-breed arced the Winchester downward and clenched his right hand around the barrel. Then powered into a half turn to aim the rifle at the fat little priest.

"Hold it, feller," he said softly.

"But . . ."

"We owe them," Edge said into the tense silence as the priest was lost for words. "Least we can do is let them do what they want."

The Orientals were angry, then puzzled. Finally impatient again.

"We understand none of this," the apparent leader of the trio said. "Just that there is trouble here. We, also, are troubled and will be so until we find Silas Martin. Good day."

He heeled his mount forward and the other two were quick to follow, cantering their horses south through the snow. The tracks they had left earlier showed their route had brought them from the north.

"You fool!" O'Keefe accused the half-breed, tears rising to the corners of his eyes as he watched the departing riders. "They were another sign."

As he suffered dismay, Angel North generated a harsh hatred, which she aimed at Edge.

"They want something as bad as you do, feller," the tall, lean man with the leveled rifle drawled. "And they had three guns against our two."

"So it wasn't anything to do with owing them anything?" Maria Lassiter asked dully, seemingly drained of the capacity to feel deep emotion.

"Way it was, both purposes were served," Edge replied evenly as he shouldered the Winchester and glanced out across the river.

Since the Orientals had ridden away, the crowd on the opposite bank had begun to disperse. A few people still stood silently on the bank. But many more were heading back up the hill toward Fallon. Some slowly. A number moving as fast as the steep and slippery slope would allow.

"Please can we go now?" Maria Lassiter asked. 'My father . . . ?"

She appeared now to be caught on the borderline between two emotions. Anxiety for the dying man in the stable of the ghost town and embarrassment that she had allowed herself to be affected by the appearance of the three Orientals.

"What's the hurry of some of those people over there?" Edge asked Karnes.

The lawman with the jug handle ears was reluctant to reply for a moment. But then he shrugged. "Some Fallon folks have got boats," he said.

"Yes," O'Keefe responded to the pregnant girl, suddenly rising above the setback. "We must leave. Come, daughter. To see the three wise men was sufficient. They were a sign."

"We ain't gotta walk all the way to that broken down old town have we, Deke?" a deputy asked miserably.

"You don't have to come if you don't want to," Angel North snarled, sharing her anger for Edge among the four lawmen. "We don't need none of you no more." She glared at Tatum. "Nor you, neither. There wasn't no doctor around the first time."

"But if you wish to see Christ reborn, you will not have to walk," the priest added with a triumphant grin. "At the house of the ferryman there are horses for all. The Almighty has provided."

"Ralph Doniphan just has the one saddle horse," Karnes said with a puzzled frown. "So how come—?"

"The Lord has provided!" O'Keefe interrupted. "For those who have faith."

"With a little help from Sam Colt," Edge said flatly, which set light to a glimmer of comprehension in the sheriff's eyes. "You already seen it ain't just religion the priest has on the brain."

Chapter Eleven

"I'LL see you all hang for this!" Sheriff Deke Karnes snarled after he had raked his shocked gaze over the carnage at the Doniphan house.

The downstream drift of the ferry had meant they had to trudge more than three hundred yards back along the river bank. This and the exertion of making the crossing had left them all breathless, the air expelled by their lungs wisping white in the air. The shock of seeing the corpses of the three Bar-M hands slumped in the snow and the blood-spattered bodies of the Doniphan family inside the house acted to deflate even more everyone except Edge, the priest, and the ex-whore.

"That's if the Faloon folks don't take the law into their own hands," Tatum added hoarsely. "The Doniphan family was well respected hereabouts."

"It was necessary," O'Keefe said, offhandedly. "They would not loan us their boat. We lost three of our own."

Edge heard the talk from the side of the house, where he had gone to reclaim his gelding and the other horses. Perhaps there were other exchanges between the divided group in front of the house, but the half-breed heard nothing more while he was in the stable at the rear, saddling the black gelding of the dead Ralph Doniphan.

When he led all the horses out to where the people

waited aboard and close to the buggy, a heavy, morbid silence was clamped over the group. Even O'Keefe and Angel North were contributing to the solemn aura. But their mood had nothing to do with the six bullet-shattered corpses close by. For their attention was directed across the river, at the town and the slope below it, where people were hurrying to drag skiffs and rowboats down to the bank.

"Ah!" the priest said gratefully as he turned to the sound of approaching hooves in the snow. "Now we can make haste. They will not be able to ferry horses across the river?"

His tone added the query and his small eyes pleaded anxiously for the reassurance of confirmation. But nobody answered him. Neither did anyone object to his suggestion that they should leave immediately.

Because the group was a mount short, the doctor elected to ride with Maria Lassiter and Redeker in the buggy. Karnes rode Doniphan's horse and his deputies swung into the saddles of the animals with Bar-M brands. The half-breed's Winchester and Remington were not drawn and O'Keefe's Colt remained inside his hat. Thus, the four lawmen moved out to start the last leg of the trip back to the ghost town of their own free will.

The verbal silence continued, the thought processes of some of the travelers written into the lines of the frowns they showed.

The pregnant girl, Redeker, and Tatum were anxious for various reasons. The sheriff and his deputies were angry at the commission of murder, their knowledge of the culprits, and their present inability to do anything about it. Angel North nurtured her hatred toward Edge. O'Keefe was eagerly excited. Edge displayed nothing on his face to hint at what was going on in his mind. Apart from the one-time Virginia City whore, it was impossible to tell whether any member of the group was still effected by the incident with the trio of Orientals.

The sun stayed bright as it inched up the cloudless dome of the sky. The mountain air was crisply cold. The direction the slow-moving group took was pre-determined by the tracks that six riders had left in the snow the previous night.

Once over the southern ridge of the east-to-west valley there was little point to backward glances, for the humps and hollows of the Wind River range would have concealed anyone who was following. But all knew that at least some of the Fallon townspeople would be moving along over the easy-to-see sign in the snow. With, among them, as many motives for reaching the ghost town as were shared by the group they were following.

Smoke smudged the sky at the head of the valley above the ghost town so that those in the buggy and riding escort knew, long before they came to a halt on the street in front of the saloon, that the livery stable out back was still occupied.

It was mid-morning by then and the cigarette papers in the half-breed's shirt pocket, sodden during the stormy river crossing, had dried out. And he separated one from the pack and rolled a smoke as he watched the activity.

"Miss Lassiter!" This from a Bar-M hand who came running down the alley between the saloon and the store.

"Dad? Is he . . . ?"

"He's still alive, Miss. But I don't know for how long."

"We have a doctor with us."

Men helped her down from the buggy and along the alley.

"Where's C.B.? And John Groves? French?"

"There was some shooting, brother."

Angel North added: "They didn't die for nothin'."
"Oh, God."
"His Son is to be born again. You know that, brother."
The voices had become faint, the words difficult to hear above the crunch of footfalls in the snow. Then the stable door was dragged open.
"Dad! Oh, Dad!"
The door was closed and a strange, eerie silence settled over the ghost town. Black smoke curled up from the stack on the stable roof. White smoke wisped from the glowing end of Edge's cigarette. The horse in the shafts of the buggy and those hitched to the rail outside the store ignored the only human presence on the street. The gelding under him waited patiently for a command.
Edge watched the eastern ridge of the valley, at the point where the trail from Fallon snaked over it. He smoked three cigarettes and the threadlike, glinting blue eyes under the hooded lids saw nothing move up there on the snow. And in all that time he heard nothing.
Then the door of the livery stable opened and footfalls crunched across the yard and along the alley.
The two Bar-M hands stepped out on to the street first. They were followed by Craig, Bassett, and Smith. Then came Karnes and his deputies. It was obvious that all the men were concerned with what was occurring back in the stable.
All of them wore deeply set frowns and were silent—in a group but strangely detached from each other. They glanced disinterestedly at Edge when Owen Craig said, "Hi, son. You come back then?"
"West was the way I was headed when all this started," the half-breed replied flatly, aware of the emptiness of the words.
"Cole Lassiter just died."

Edge nodded. "So the girl got what she wanted."

"Better than that, even. He managed to nod that it was all right with him for her to marry Redeker. Priest is doin' the ceremony now."

After a glance at Edge, Craig had joined the others in peering down the alley toward the livery stable door.

The half-breed continued to watch the trail over the ridge. "Didn't they want witnesses, feller?"

"Ain't that son. Touch and go which comes first. The couple bein' married or the baby arrivin'. Wouldn't be right for all of us to be there for the baby bein' born."

He took out his pipe and clamped the stem between his teeth, to suck at the emptiness of the bowl.

"Right for them to be around, I guess," Edge said.

The others seemed not to be aware of the talk. But their attention was suddenly captured when Craig followed the direction of the half-breed's nod and gasped: "Holy cow! They what they look like?"

Everyone stared up to the crest of the high ground in the east and saw the trio of riders who had halted there. Even though they were no more than dark silhouettes against the sun-bright sky, their exotic garb of strangely shaped hats and flowing robes could be recognized by the men who had seen them before.

"The three Kings from the Orient!" Karnes confirmed huskily.

"They're headin' south!" This from the deputy named Frank as the men on the ridge wheeled their mounts.

The sheepmen stared disconsolately at the departing riders, then anxiously at Edge.

"They oughta be here," Smith groaned. "Couldn't you go—"

"Looking for a feller called Silas Martin," the half-breed answered absently as he gazed pensively after the trio of Japanese. "Guess the river trail was blocked."

All attention was abruptly drawn back to the stable out back of the saloon as the door was flung open and running footfalls sounded.

"It's started!" O'Keefe exclaimed, his fleshy face bright crimson with excitement as he reached the buggy and began to delve beneath the blanket on the footboard. "The baby's coming! It won't be easy for her! She'll have to be cut!" His features were abruptly contorted by a frown of almost painful anguish. "What happened to Tatum's bag?"

The hard silence that followed his cry as he flung the blanket to the snow was ended by a shuddering moan from Maria Lassiter. Then a shrill scream.

Edge pushed a hand into the long hair at the nape of his neck. He drew the razor from the pouch and closed the blade into the handle before he called: "Here, priest. Be a change for it to give life instead of taking it. I want it back right after." He tossed the closed razor and O'Keefe caught it instinctively in his pudgy hands. "Don't come back without it, feller."

O'Keefe nodded, whirled, and raced back along the alley.

"What the hell happened to the doc's—?" a deputy started.

"Lost back at the river, probably," the sheriff suggested dully as the stable door was closed again, muting the harsh sounds of the pregnant woman's labor. "We had to get off that ferry pretty damn fast."

The subject was immediately forgotten as the weary eyes of men who had been without sleep for a long time returned to peer at the east ridge. But the trio of riders had gone from sight.

"They was supposed to bring gifts," Bassett growled.

"Damn the heathen bastards!" the deputy named Frank snarled. "We don't need 'em. I got my gold watch I can give the baby. Sheriff?"

Karnes delved into a pants pocket and brought out

some loose change. "I didn't count on takin' no trip today. I just got a dollar, Frank. In cents."

"That'll be okay. Anyone else?"

The other two deputies, the trio of sheepmen, and the two Bar-M hands shook their heads.

"Nothin' it'd be fittin' to give a new born baby," Smith said miserably.

They all looked up at the mounted Edge. "I ain't never found need to carry any myrrh," he told them.

Every face showed a scowl, which was then snatched off the fatigued, bristled features by the familiar sound of the stable door being opened.

The priest came down the alley: slowly this time, head bowed. When he reached the street and looked up he showed a face wreathed with an expression of awe.

"He will be reborn very soon, brothers," he whispered. "Let us pray."

As he dropped to his knees and brought his hands together at his chin, he realized he was carrying the razor. He held it out and Edge rode up close to him to reach down and take it.

"Obliged," the half-breed said as the other men on the street sank to their knees and assumed attitudes of prayer.

"Your help is greatly appreciated, sir," O'Keefe said, with a sincerity of tone and expression, which for the first time caused him to sound and look like a genuine priest.

Edge nodded and pulled the blade from the handle before he replaced the razor in the pouch. It was still warm, probably from boiling water rather than the girl's flesh.

Then he heeled the horse forward, turning to ride across the street and between the two houses at the start of the southwest trail. Behind him, O'Keefe spoke softly and reverently. Far to his left, there was movement again on the eastern rim of the valley. Not riders this time. People on foot trudging through the snow. Many more than three of them. The citizens of Fallon nearing the end of their long walk from the Wind River.

Edge ignored them and found this easy to do. It was not so simple to detach himself from what was happening in the stable. To do that he had to think determinedly materialistic thoughts about an unknown man named Silas Martin. To concentrate on the three Japanese who were looking for him. And to consider how he might capitalize on their search.

He rode slowly, not conscious of any reluctance to leave the ghost town behind. Aware only that he had to make a great effort to confine his thoughts to what lay ahead.

It was a quarter of a mile south when something in the snow caught his attention and he reined the gelding to a halt. He swung down from the saddle as he recognized the warped and rotting timber of a town marker board, half buried in the snow. As he used a booted foot to clear the flakes away from the faded lettering, he glanced up the slope.

The people from Fallon had reached the ghost town and were moving silently along the street.

He looked down at the town marker and read: WELCOME TO BETH. His vision was suddenly blurred by the threat of tears. Of grief for a long dead wife? A vivid mental image of a woman's face with maggots crawling out over the lips flashed through his mind. Of regret that she had not survived long enough to bear a child?

He shook his head violently, making a physical effort to clear his mind of other haunting images. A tear spilled from each cracked open eye and coursed down the dark, lined, cold-pinched, bristled flesh of his face.

The plaintive first cry of a new-born baby floated

down the slope from the ghost town, which was now crowded with a waiting throng.

"Jesus Christ!" a man roared.

A moment of utter silence.

The voice of Joseph Redeker announced: "It's a girl! Thank God it's a girl!"

Edge swept his foot to the side to reveal the entire marker board: WELCOME TO BETHEL.

A bedlam of hysterical shouting and screaming exploded from the town: the body of sound rushing down the snow-cloaked valley. As he swung astride the gelding again, Edge could distinguish no single word. But the tone of the massed voices was of depthless rage.

Then he saw a flurry of movement between the two houses where the southwest trail began. And he laid a hand on the stock of his booted Winchester as angry people filled the gap. But they advanced only as far as the rear of the houses, there to divide into two groups.

The screams and shouts continued at a constant volume. But amid the shrillness there was now a sound of lower pitch—a regular *thud, thud, thud, thud.* Like powerful hammer blows.

Edge watched the frantic crowds impassively, unable to recognize individuals through the dazzle of reflected light of the noon sun striking the snow.

Then a rider appeared between the houses. And was allowed to head down the trail unhindered.

The half-breed gripped the Winchester again and maintained his hold on the rifle even after he recognized the rider as Joe Redeker. As the youngster rode up to the half-breed and reined his mount to a halt, the citizens of Fallon fell silent and moved into a single group again: in the gap at the start of the trail. And Edge was able to see how they had expunged their rage.

It had been hammer blows he heard amid the raised voices, driving nails through the hands and feet of

O'Keefe and Angel North. For the priest and the one-time Virginia City whore had been crucified—spread-eagled against the rear walls of the houses. The blood from their wounds showed clearly. Their heads were hung forward, chins resting on their chests. If they were conscious and venting their agony, the sounds were not loud enough to reach Edge.

"It's for the killin' of the ferryman and his family," Redeker supplied grimly after a grimacing glance over his shoulder. "Somebody said it would be a fittin' way for them to die."

"Just through the hands and feet?" Edge asked. "Nowhere else?"

"No. They'll be a long time dyin'. Some of the folks liked that. I come to tell you thanks, Mr. Edge. For yesterday. And for helpin' to get Maria to her pa before he died. Best you don't come back. Them people back there know you did some of the shootin' at the Doniphan house."

"Obliged, kid," the half-breed said, and drew the Winchester from the boot. "But I can do what I have to do from here."

Redeker vented a gasp of shock as Edge pumped the action of the rifle, thudded the stock to his shoulder and squeezed off a shot. Then pumped, raked the barrel to the side, and fired again.

The hanging forms of Angel North and O'Keefe each jerked once and became inert.

An angry roar exploded from the crowd.

The drifting gunsmoke disintegrated and its acrid taint was neutralized by the ice cold air.

The crowd stirred into movement, then became still again. Perhaps sick of killing. Or maybe realizing that the half-breed was too far away to be caught.

Redeker cleared his throat. "They were crazy, but they believed some kinda miracle was goin' to happen here today. So did a lot of Fallon folks. I think maybe it not happenin' made them people even more mad than the killin' at the Doniphan house. I'm glad you ended their sufferin', Mr. Edge."

"So am I, kid," the half-breed answered evenly as he slid the rifle back into the boot and made to wheel his horse.

"For awhile there, they had me believin' it," Redeker said huskily. Then he showed a wan, exhausted grin of relief. "But I should've known. It was the first time for both of us. Maria and me. With each other or anyone else. It was over before we knew it, almost. But I know I was inside her when it happened for me. And she bled like she was supposed to. So I knew it was no immaculate conception, Mr. Edge."

"No sweat, kid," the half-breed drawled as he tugged on the reins to turn the gelding south. "You'll both improve with practice."